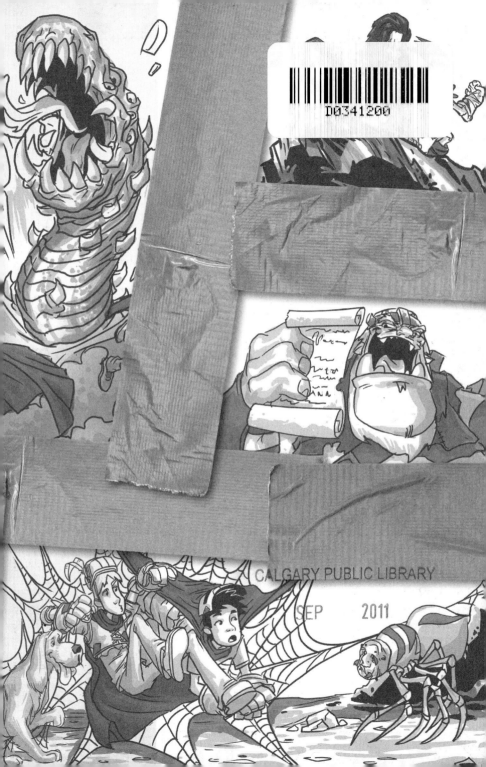

SIR SETH
THISTLETHWAITE
and the Kingdom of the Caves

Sir Ollie   Sir Seth   and Shasta

Written by Richard Thake
Illustrated by Vince Chui

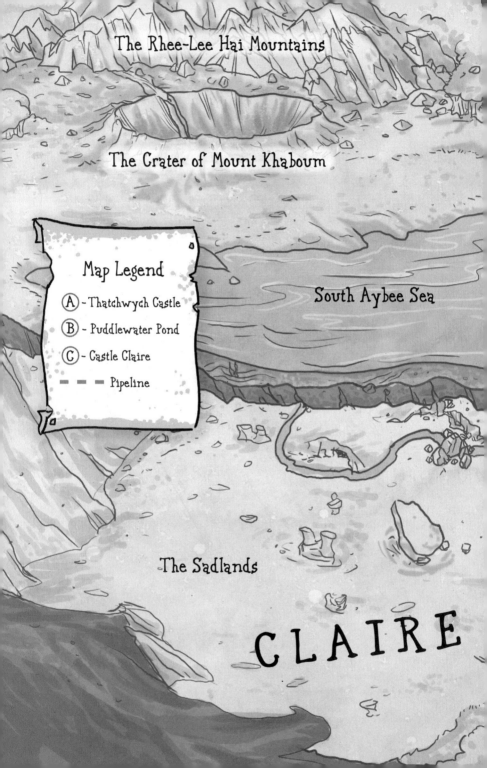

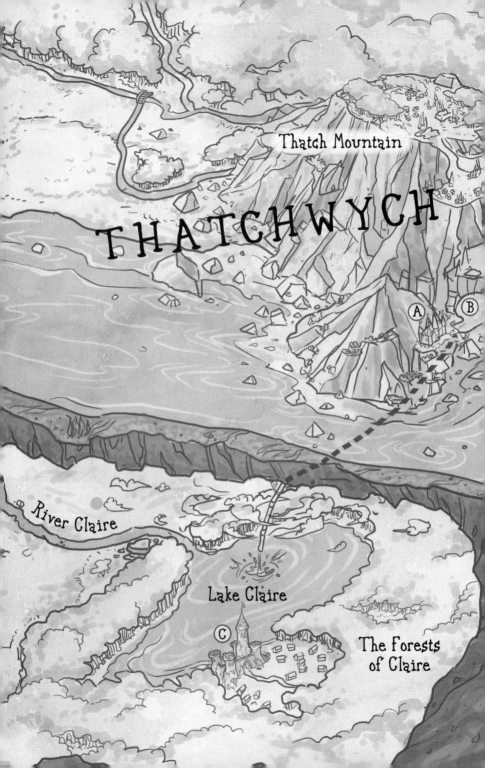

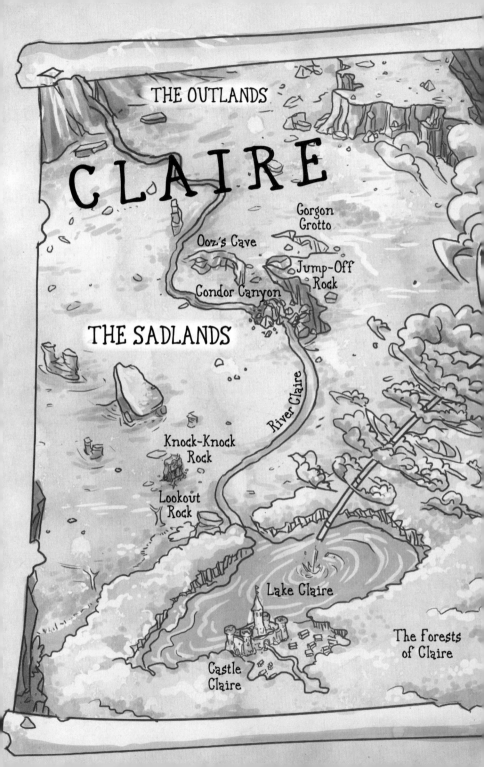

Queen Beatrix the Sixth

Princess Sundra Neeth

Pho Phum

Phi Phum

Phee Phum

Oor, the evil, awful elf

Grak, the Snactisaurus rex

Glug, the chuggamugga bug

Buzz, the umbie

Saffron, the gorgon

Owlkids Books Inc.
10 Lower Spadina Avenue, Suite 400, Toronto, Ontario M5V 2Z2
www.owlkids.com

Library and Archives Canada Cataloguing in Publication

Thake, Richard, 1938-
         Sir Seth Thistlethwaite and the kingdom of the caves / Richard Thake,
Vince Chui.

Issued also in electronic format.
ISBN 978-1-926818-94-8 (bound).--ISBN 978-1-926818-95-5 (pbk.)

         I. Chui, Vince, 1975- II. Title.

PS8639.H36S565 2011   jC813'.6   C2011-900261-2

Library of Congress Control Number: 2010943316

Design: Barb Kelly

**Canada Council
for the Arts**

**Conseil des Arts
du Canada**

**ONTARIO ARTS COUNCIL
CONSEIL DES ARTS DE L'ONTARIO**

We acknowledge the financial support of the Canada Council for the Arts, the
Ontario Arts Council, the Government of Canada through the Canada Book
Fund (CBF), and the Government of Ontario through the Ontario Media
Development Corporation's Book Initiative for our publishing activities.

Manufactured by Friesens Corporation
Manufactured in Altona, MB, Canada in March 2011
Job #63855

A   B   C   D   E   F

Mixed Sources

Cert no. SW-COC-001271
© 1996 FSC

FSC

CONTENTS

1 To Puddlewater Pond

Seth Thistlethwaite didn't know how he knew that he knew it, but from somewhere inside his still-sleeping mind, a small voice began to whisper: Hey Seth, morning's just about here. Time to get up and get going...

He cautiously opened one eye, and sure enough, out there in the dew-dappled distance, the yellowish fringe of first light was ever so slowly tiptoeing into the night. It crept past the still-twinkling stars, announcing that another new wonder-filled day was getting ready to get under way.

Seth threw back the covers, but before his feet had even touched the floor, he was suddenly Seth Thistlethwaite no more. In his stead, from his bed, arose none other than Sir Seth Thistlethwaite, that fearless and famous ten-year-old knight of far-flung legend and renown—who, brandishing a broomstick broadsword fashioned from sturdy birch and clad in shin pads and hockey gloves of the finest spray-painted silver, joined his very best friend, Sir Ollie Everghettz, to form that noble band of adventurous crusaders known throughout the land as the Mighty Knights of Right & Honor!

However, before he could go galloping gallantly forth into the exciting, soaring world of his rich imagination, Sir Seth realized something of great importance: he had completely forgotten to wake up and saddle his horse! For there, gloriously snoring on the end of his bed, lay his faithful steed, Shasta, who, in the hazy half light between morning and night, looked more like a smiley golden retriever than she did a horse.

"Hey, Shasta," Sir Seth said, leaning down and whispering into one ear. "Wake up, girl. It's time for us to suit up and ride. And I think I may have just seen a squirrel out there..."

Squirrel! That was the magic word. Shasta was instantly wide-eyed awake. Her eyes popped open as she scrambled to find her feet—the way most horses do when they hear the word "squirrel."

Sir Seth smoothed the rumpled mop of fur on top of her head. "C'mon, girl, we don't want to be late. Sir Ollie's going to meet us by the blueberry bushes down by Puddlewater Pond!"

And so, after a lightning-fast breakfast—and quick armor touch-up with some fresh, shiny strips of silver duct tape—Sir Seth and Shasta ducked through the two loose boards at the far end of the fence and headed out to an old, unmown, almost overgrown, and largely unknown lost little pathway—one that twists and turns some twenty-two times as it wends its way down to the yummy, summery waters of Puddlewater Pond.

And somewhere along the way down that long, grassy trail, Sir Seth and Shasta crossed over that invisible line between the world of what's real and that magical, wonder-filled world of imagination.

The moment they did, they immediately found themselves under the always cloudless and blue skies of that very old, merry old, frightfully, delightfully old cuckoo-clock Kingdom of Thatchwych.

When you get there, the first thing you'll notice this time of year are the frilly bubblegum chrysanthemums nestled everywhere among the shy, dark-eyed oopsah daisies. And way up high, in the tops of the jellybean trees, the orange and red blossoms are in full bloom, announcing to the world that it's another magnificent day to be a Mighty Knight—just like Sir Seth's fellow knight, Sir Ollie. There he stood, eating freshly picked blueberries in the shade of a big old elm tree where their home-crafted raft, the *Mighty Voyager*, was basking by the shore in the soft morning sun.

The minute he saw Ollie, Sir Seth signaled to Shasta to stay. Like a silently shifting shadow, he drifted around behind his best friend, then shinnied up one of the huge old elm trees that towered above the water. On the big bottom branch of the tree closest to the water, they had tied a long rope so they could swing from the tree behind it out over the pond. Sir Seth took the rope in both hands, pushed off, and on the way by, hollered at the top of his lungs...

"HEY, Ollieeeeeeeeee! It's time to ride!"

Sir Ollie jumped straight up into the still morning air and swallowed two unchewed blueberries the size of your thumb as Sir Seth went breezing by in a blur.

"Whoo!! What a good 'Gotcha!'" he spluttered around the beginning of a grin. "Good thing you weren't a dino or rhino or somethin' double-dangerous like that."

They immediately clasped their hands in the triple-mega-secret Mighty Knights' handshake, then raised their swords and repeated the Mighty Knights' motto:

"A Mighty Knight will do whatever he must to take a wrong and make it a right!"

Then the two friends quickly slipped on their lifejackets, shoved the *Mighty Voyager* into the warm waiting waters of the large pond, and hopped on.

"Ready, Sir Ollie?"

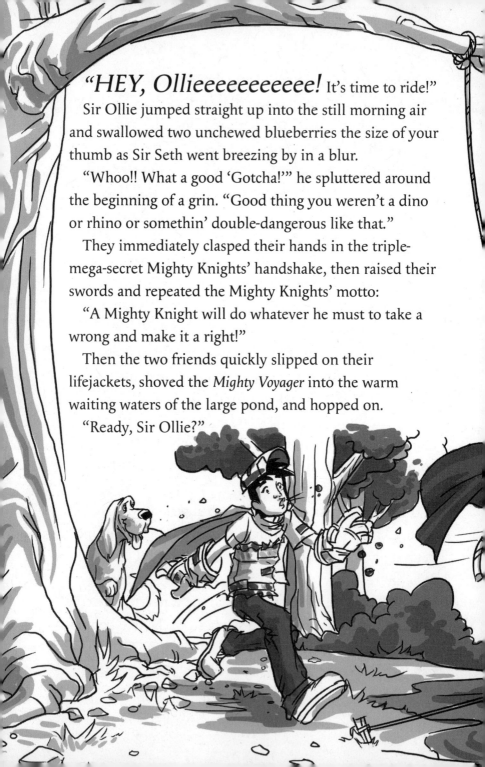

"Ready, Sir Seth," he replied, climbing onto one of the two old bicycles Seth's father had bolted to the middle of the raft. When Sir Seth and Sir Ollie pedaled, the chains turned an underwater wooden propeller, which made their raft the only pedal-powered rotary craft anywhere in all of Thatchwych. And if that wasn't neat enough, the handlebars also turned an underwater rudder, so you could go wherever you wanted. Then, if you hoisted the old bedsheet up the mast, the *Mighty Voyager* turned into a sailboat. It was just too two-way cool to be true.

"C'mon, Shasta," Sir Seth called, helping her clamber aboard. "You're a Mighty Knight, too."

With a good shake, she sprayed them with an explosion of sunshiny water. Sir Seth hopped on the other bike, and together the two friends pedaled their

ramshackle raft out toward the middle of the pond.

"Hey, Seth..." Sir Ollie began while popping a handful of blueberries into his mouth.

"Yeah?" his friend said lazily.

"D'you think the water looks...uh, sorta lower than it was yesterday?"

Sir Seth perked up and glanced over at Ollie. "Yeah. Y'know, when I saw the *Voyager* this morning, she was sitting halfway out of the water. I wonder how come?"

They looked at each other, then at the water, trying to guess what the answer might be.

Then, with a huge GUH–LUMPH, a bulbous bubble even bigger than old Mister Mittermeyer's falling-down barn rumbled up under the *Mighty Voyager* and rocked it back and forth like a toy boat in a bathtub.

For a moment, the pond went heart-stoppingly still... until six seconds later, when another, even bigger bubble GUH–LUMPHED up fiercely from below.

"Wh-wh-what was that?" Sir Ollie stuttered with surprise, his eyes the size of banana cream pies (which is the standard measurement of everything in Thatchwych).

Sir Seth looked back with nervous eyes the same size. "I don't know. I've never seen bubbles that big before."

Sir Ollie immediately reached for El Gonzo, his Mighty Knightly sword. "It could only be one thing: a giant sea serpent!!"

"A sea serpent?!" Sir Seth gasped.

"In Puddlewater Pond?"

"Don't you know anything about sea serpents? They always roar under water like that just before they attack," Ollie explained, peering down into the water. "That's what all those bubbles are from."

"Yeah?" Sir Seth flopped down beside his friend. "Can you actually see the sea serpent down there?"

"Well, no," said Sir Ollie, standing back up, "but I see something up there! Up in the sky. Twelve o'clock high."

Sure enough, directly overhead, a strange silhouetted bird was circling slowly. While the two knights looked on, it folded its wings and started straight down, as though to dive-bomb the raft. That's when Shasta saw it too and began whoo-whoo-whooing in excited circles.

"To arms, to arms!" Sir Seth drew his sword as yet another HUGE bubble rocked their rolling raft. "We're being attacked by a giant bird up above and a slithering sea serpent down below—at the same time! Sir Ollie, you take the sea serpent. I'll take the bird."

Sir Ollie thought about it briefly. "Um, how come I get the sea serpent and you get the bird?"

"Because the tough ones are the only ones that Everghettz ever gets—or so I've heard." Sir Seth smiled.

Sir Ollie didn't.

"Yeah, I've heard that, too," he groaned. "I hear it every time you come to a tough one."

"Hey, if you don't think you can handle it," shrugged Sir Seth, "I'll take the sea serpent. You can take the bird."

Sir Ollie scowled and swished his sword swiftly. "Me? Can't handle some dumb old sea serpent? I doubt it!"

But by now, the plummeting bird was nearly upon them. The two Mighty Knights braced themselves as they watched it level out just above the water and—at roughly warp speed—come streaking right toward them!

"On second thought," cried Sir Ollie as he stood beside his friend, "I think we should both take the bird!"

And then, at the last second, the giant bird swerved and shot past the *Mighty Voyager*—all while lying on its back, peeling a banana, and shouting something like: "Hey, cuzzins, guess who? Good to see you agaaaaain!"

Sir Seth gaped at Sir Ollie. Sir Ollie gaped at Sir Seth. This was no bird but a rather spectacular sloth named...

"Edith-Anne!"

Together the two knights expressed their excitement—and relief—at the sight of their fantastically furry friend. They could hardly wait for her to land.

"Clear the deck, cuzzins!" the streaking sloth called down as she swept up in a circle, preparing to land. She was excitedly waving a rolled-up scroll.

"I wonder what that could be?" Sir Ollie asked.

"We'll know in a sec, I suppose," replied Sir Seth.

But if the Mighty Knights had puzzled for the next two thousand and thirty-two years, they'd have never, never, ever guessed that rolled-up scroll would send them deep down, down, down to a unknown underground world...

A world where no Thatchwychian soul had ever been.

2

The Mysterious Mission

"Edith-Anne!" said Sir Seth with large grin. "Are we ever glad to see it's you!"

"Yeah! And not some huge knight-gobbling hawk!" cried Sir Ollie. "But what are you doing here?"

Edith-Anne winked and excitedly began unrolling a Royal Thatchwychian scroll marked:

SECRET! URGENT! FOR MIGHTY KNIGHTS ONLY!

which meant it could only have come from King Philip Fluster the Fourth himself.

"I bring a message from the king!" said Edith-Anne gleefully. "That's right: I'm the official Royal Runner!"

Now, I know what you're thinking. Why would a king as regal as King Philip Fluster the Fourth want someone as astonishingly sluggish and slow as a sloth to be his official Royal Runner? Well, there are, in fact, a couple of very good reasons for that.

Number one: Edith-Anne can speak thirty-three of the known Thatchwychian languages, including Middle, Lower, and Southernmost Thatch; Bogglegab; Isoceleeze; Hypotheceeze; and several other "eezes" that sound much like sneezes. And number two: although she's not much of a walker, she's actually a super-fast flyer—if she has enough of her magic sloth broth on hand. With a rare pair of messenger skills such as these, you can certainly and suddenly see why anyone, anywhere would want to have Edith-Anne as a runner. Even if she can't really run.

"So, cuzzins?" she asked. "Are you saddled up and ready for your next knightly assignment?"

Just then, the biggest bubble of all burst with a giant GUH-LUMPH, knocking Sir Seth into Sir Ollie, who was in turn knocked into Shasta, who was in turn nearly knocked into the water!

"Ready," Sir Seth said, regaining his feet.

"Ready," Sir Ollie also said. "But let's hurry!"

Edith-Anne nodded. "Okay, cuzzins. The message says:

'By royal decree, be it known to one and all that
the Mighty Knights of Right & Honor are, herewith,
duly and truly directed to stop the water from draining
out of Puddlewater Pond.

With many thanks,
King Philip the Fourth of Thatchwych.'"

Sir Seth looked over at Sir Ollie in open-mouthed awe. "Stop the water? But there's a sea serpent down there! Just how do we do that?"

Just then, another gigantic GUH-LUMPH bubbled up, almost in response.

"Well, I don't think you just walk up to one and say 'shoo,'" Sir Ollie smiled nervously.

"Whoa, whoa!" Edith-Anne cocked her head just so.

"Did you just say s-s-sea serpent?! Are you sure?"

"Seems like it." Sir Seth nodded. "But serpent or no serpent, we gotta solve this mystery! For the king!"

Then, like the true Mighty Knight he was, Sir Ollie stood tall and shouted: "This looks like another tough one for Everghettz! Excuse me, but I'd better go down there and tell that serpent to find some other pond to guh-lumph in." He grinned shyly at Sir Seth. "Um, feel free to come with me—if you think you can handle it."

Sir Seth smiled and slapped his friend on the back. "We'll need our UBHs."

When she heard that word, Shasta automatically ran over and brought them their underwater goggles.

For those of you who don't already know, a UBH is a magical Underwater Breathing Hose. And as Mighty Knights, Sir Seth and Sir Ollie both have one, of course. They each attach one end to top of the mast on the raft—that way, they can breathe in and out when they're walking around under the water.

When they were geared up and ready to go, Sir Ollie looked down into the muddy green water. "Where do you think the serpent is?"

"Those bubbles are coming straight up," said Sir Seth, "so I'd say it's on the bottom, right under the raft."

"Let's find out," Sir Ollie said, huffing into his hose to make sure it was clear. "Ready?"

"Yep. Let's go slay us a sea serpent!" Sir Seth smiled back. He looked up at Edith-Anne. "Can you stay here with Shasta? We've only got two UBHs."

"Well, cuzzins," Edith-Anne said, "maybe I oughta fly back and tell the king. You might need reinforcements."

"Yeah, that's a good idea!" Sir Seth agreed. "But you'd better be quick! We gotta get going, before the Puddlewater Pond runs out of water."

"Okay, I'll be back," said Edith-Anne. "Good luck... and be careful down there!" And with that, she spread her long arms, jumped into the air, and was away.

Sir Seth and Sir Ollie pulled down their goggles and slid off the *Mighty Voyager* into the warm water. And immediately,

everything turned from bright yellow sunshine to the soft, hushed slow-motion world under Puddlewater Pond, where even the rushes are in no particular hurry.

At least, that's what Sir Seth saw. Sir Ollie, however, got his foot tangled in the UBH and did a fabulous full forward bellyflop face first into the pond—swallowing about two bucketfuls of rich green Puddlewater water as he did. That sometimes happens to knights when they're in a hurry. So he had to grab the raft and blow out his hose all over again.

Which left his friend Sir Seth all alone!

Sir Ollie frantically cleared his hose and dove back down after Sir Seth. It took his eyes several seconds to adjust to the lazily undulating watery world below. But ah! There was Sir Seth. Still alive and waiting for him.

With his UBH clamped firmly in his fist, Sir Ollie swan-dove to his friend and exchanged a thumb-and-finger "OK" sign with his other hand. The two Mighty Knights took a good look around—no sign of the sea serpent anywhere. Sir Seth pointed down with one hand to suggest they dive deeper into the murky pond.

Sir Ollie was about to give his friend another "OK" when an enooooormous bubble half the size of Puddlewater Pond suddenly came belching up with a great, gushing freight-train-like rush and a deafening...

GUH-LUMPH!!!

...just like when you pull out the plug in a bath tub.

Tumbling head over heels out of control, Sir Seth and

Sir Ollie—helplessly, hopelessly—looked at each other in shock and awe. If he could, Sir Seth surely would have said, "Another fine mess we've gotten into, Sir Ollie!"

But before they could say or do anything at all, the two Mighty Knights could feel themselves being drawn down, down, down to the bottom of the pond. Could this evil sea serpent be sucking them into its wide, waiting jaws for lunch?

Sir Seth quickly drew his sword and looked down. But there was nothing to see through the bubbly waters. No swirling shape of sea serpent in sight! He glanced over at Sir Ollie, who was kicking as hard as he could, trying to go back up to the raft. But the invisible force kept pulling the two friends farther and farther down, down, down...

In a cloud of swirling mud, Sir Seth's feet hit bottom with a thud. Desperately, he found a tangle of reeds, weeds and an old submerged tree to grab onto. Sir Ollie dropped down beside Sir Seth and also grabbed a fistful of reeds and weeds. Yet still, that invisible force relentlessly kept pulling him and his friend closer and closer—but closer to what?

Then, without warning, everything stopped.

Puddlewater Pond went as still and serene as it was before. The two shocked knights looked at each other. And then they looked around. Still no sea serpent. Or much of anything else. Sir Ollie anxiously began pointing up. Sir Seth nodded—after all, soon Edith-Anne would arrive with royal reinforcements from Thatchwych.

But just as the friends were about to head up to the surface, a huge hole opened directly beneath their feet and swallowed both of the Mighty Knights in one gigantic, gurgling, bubbling...

GUH-LUMPH!!!

And with that, in the blink of an eye, the Mighty Knights disappeared right out of sight.

But where had they gone?

3 Just Where Is Claire?

When you get there, you'll find everything about Claire is unusually rare. For one thing, Claire's the only kingdom you'll find anywhere that has a queen as its king. But the rareness of Claire doesn't end there. Because Claire is neither here nor there, or anywhere else you can see. It's "down there"—way, way down, far below the ground. It's a place so unknown and completely alone and bizarre, not even the people who live there know exactly where they are.

This underground kingdom of the caves began a long time ago, when moody Mount Khaboum was just a simmering volcano somewhere over in the Rhee Li Hai Mountains. Then, one day in the middle of May, Mount Khaboum threw a hissy volcanic fit and blew its snowy top all over the neighboring nation of Yubet. Which made the Rhee Li Hai Mountains quite a bit higher. But didn't do much for moody Mount Khaboum.

When the smoke and ashes had finally settled, all that was left of that grumpy old mountain was some sizzling snow, a small rainbow, and quite a large hole in the ground. For the first time in millions of years, life-giving sunshine began streaming into and through all the drab, dreary caves huddled together down there in the dark.

And at that magic moment—the same day the first ray of sunshine touched the cold black rock for the very first time—the kingdom of Claire became the only country anywhere to be found that's located completely under the ground. And which, quite by chance, is directly below what we've all come to know as Puddlewater Pond!

Following the sunshine under the ground came shivering, quivering Khaboumian nomads, who wandered in through the still-smoldering snow to become the first people of Claire. (Now, all Khaboumians were and are quite short—because when you live in a country as cold as Khaboum, the shorter you are, the less of you there is to get cold. Even today, the grown-ups in Claire are all still just four feet tall, no less, no more.)

And so it went, for hundreds and thousands of years—the sunshine shone in on that brand-new, grand-new land down below, warming the gathering soil for mile after awakening mile in every direction. Even the meandering River Claire made its lazily winding way down through the middle, filled with pickerel and perch and crayfish and frogs—waiting, no doubt, for the Mighty Knights to come riding by with their dog.

Everything, everywhere in the gradually greening kingdom of Claire was so gloriously grand that the people of Claire were—and still are to this day—utterly unaware that they really live in a big hole in the ground. But even if they knew that, they really wouldn't care. Everything they need is right there. Down there in Claire.

However, the kingdom of Claire wouldn't be as wondrously rare as it is today, in every imaginable way, if it hadn't been for the wisdom of good Queen Claire, who was the first queen of the kingdom. Having a queen as a king could have been confusing for everyone there. But good Queen Claire decided, then and there, that the country should be known as the Queendom of Claire.

Which helped for a while, until Queen Claire's first-born son—also named Claire—became the king...and switched the queendom back to a kingdom all over again!

And so the name changed from queendom to kingdom for reign after reign, until one day when Queen Claire the Tenth decided that enough was enough. So she took the great Magna Charter—the sacred document that even now announces and pronounces the name of the rightful monarch of Claire—and wrote upon it "The Queendom of Claire." Then she locked the charter in a tall glass cask. And as queen, only she kept the key.

Ever since then, this kingdom of the caves has forever been known as the quite quaint Queendom of Claire.

Which brings us to the wise Queen Beatrix the Sixth, who rules Claire today. That's her signature you'll find at the bottom of the magnificent Magna Charter. Just as it always had blissfully been. Only now, Queen Beatrix's queendom found itself much less blissful than it was normally known to be.

"Gentlemen," the queen began, addressing the assembled royal engineers in a voice that rattled the windows at the far end of the castle, "the reason I called all of you here today is...we have a problem!"

26

"A problem, Your Majesty?" Ed, the head engineer, said uneasily. "Uh, what problem is that?"

Queen Beatrix leaned forward and stared deep into his eyes. "A sudden, unexplained landslide has blocked the River Claire somewhere up there by Jump-Off Rock. The self-same river that daily brings water rushing into our grand Lake Claire. Unless you unblock all these rocks—and do it without delay—our Lake Claire could one day be bare." She rose back up to her full height. "This queendom could find itself gasping and rasping, without any water!"

A giant gasp escaped from the engineers' mouths. Ed was about to answer his queen when Sir Duncan, the

queen's chief confidant and adviser, hurried into the meeting and whispered nervously into her ear.

"Your Majesty, I do apologize for interrupting such an important meeting, but that evil, awful elf from the Sadlands, Ooz"—he said this last word with a shudder, as though it tasted like worms in his mouth—"is here and demands to see you at once."

"Ooz?! Doesn't he realize we have a water problem?" Queen Bea snorted. "Have him come back tomorrow."

Sir Duncan leaned closer. "I think perhaps you might want to have a word him, Your Majesty. It seems the reason we have a water problem in Claire is because Ooz has blocked the river."

"Ooz blocked the river?" the queen repeated. She coughed softly and sat down with a sigh on her throne. "Thank you, Sir Duncan," she sighed, as though she, too, had the taste of worms in her mouth. She turned to the assembled royal engineers. "Gentlemen, you can discuss our water problem in that room over there while I meet with Mister Ooz. In the meantime, Sir Duncan, please summon the Council of Elders. Have them come here at once. And..."

Sir Duncan, who was already halfway out of the room, stopped in his tracks.

"Have Princess Sundra Neeth join us as well."

"Yes, Your Majesty"—Sir Duncan bowed—"if we can find her. She seems to have disappeared. Again."

Queen Bea sighed all over again. "Have you looked

under the counters in the kitchen?" she suggested. "She loves to put the mousetrap down there as a little surprise when the chef reaches in for a pot or a pan."

"That was the first place we looked, Your Majesty."

"Well, did you look under the laundry? And in the chandelier in the sitting room? Or inside Sir Cecil's suit of armor?" the queen queried quickly.

"Your Majesty, the entire castle staff has looked here and there and everywhere. But the princess is simply nowhere to be found."

The queen sighed one last sigh. "Perhaps the Royal Dining Room. Did you think to look there?"

This time, it was Sir Duncan's turn to sigh. "Well, the princess had definitely been there because there was sugar in the salt shakers and salt in the sugar bowls. But she was gone by the time we got there."

"Then look again!" the queen roared. "If she ever expects to rule this country, she'll need to know how to solve problems like these."

Slowly, the queen got to her feet and walked over to the open windows overlooking the green, green Royal Claireberry Gardens. The sun was dancing like freshly cut diamonds on the crystal clear waters of lovely Lake Claire. And everywhere one looked, there were flocks of flitting finches serenading the sky from the blossoming branches of all the tall, towering Claireberry trees. Everything outside her window was so utterly and delightfully right.

But was all this about to come to an end?

Things weren't so fair everywhere in Claire. Because just over there, beyond the far edge of Lake Claire, begins the bare area known as the Sadlands—a barren, windswept desert where only nomads and condors can survive. All because of Grak and his unending appetite for trees.

Who or what is Grak, you might ask? Well, he's the biggest thing anywhere in the entire Queendom of Claire—a massive, mountainous tree-eating dino that the evil little Ooz keeps as his personal pet.

"Your Majesty"—Sir Duncan's voice broke her thoughts—"Mister Ooz is quite insistent..."

"I don't know exactly what evil plotting has driven that vile little elf to block our beloved river," Queen Beatrix replied, seating herself once again on her throne, "but I am still Queen of Claire! He can wait in the anteroom with my uncle for my arrival."

"HA! What do you mean, 'He can wait'?" a gruff voice growled from the tall, ornate door of the Great Hall. "I wait for no one."

"Mister Ooz, how delightful to see you," the queen gushed, barely disguising her distaste—being royal demanded such politeness. "And just what, may I ask, brings you to Castle Claire on this wondrous day?"

The very sight of him made the queen shudder. Ooz was so hairy and scary and utterly awful, from the tips of his toes to the three-haired wart on the end of his nose, all the gnats, rats, and bats had long ago packed up and left his cave in disgust. Fleas and flies would fly right on by rather than taking a bite of that gruesome green skin. In fact, Ooz was so frighteningly haunting and daunting, he could actually gag a maggot, so some people say, with just one look of those crooked yellow eyes.

Everything about Ooz was also unusually small— because, overall, he was only two feet, two inches tall. Which meant the arrows he kept in the pack on his back were just one foot long so they wouldn't drag on the ground wherever he walked. His sword and his shoes, his coat and his hat were also the same size as that. Everything about him was teeny and weeny. And mean.

He strode over and jumped up onto the windowsill. "What brings me to Claire? Look there." Ooz pointed one of the axes that he wielded wherever he went.

Queen Beatrix smiled without smiling, not wanting to get any closer. "Perhaps you could just tell me what you see—and save me the trip."

"I see trees!" Ooz growled.

"Trees. Yes, go on..."

"And flowers! And grass!" Ooz growled again.

"Yes, yes...um, is there a problem with that?" the queen wondered out loud.

"YES!" the little man bellowed so loud he almost blew the Council of Elders back out through the door they had just entered. "I want the Sadlands to look just like that!"

"If you hadn't chopped down all the trees up there, the Sadlands would still be as green as that," Sir Duncan dared to remind him.

"Don't blame me! It's my dino, Grak. He never stops eating—and all he ever eats are trees, peas, and knights!" Ooz, in turn, angrily reminded Sir Duncan. "And since there are no peas and no knights up there anymore, that leaves only trees. And even they are just about gone. And when they are, the only food for Grak will be rocks."

As quick as a wink and before you could think, Ooz whirled and hurled his ax, which embedded itself in the door beside Sir Duncan's unsuspecting head.

"But of course, you already know this, Your Majesty," Ooz snarled. "By your order, Claire's army has blocked Grak's path! Tell them to step aside and allow Grak to pass—or forever afterward, live with my wrath!"

"Your wrath?" The queen was now truly losing her

patience. "I warn you, sir, you don't know what wrath means...until you've felt mine!"

Ooz smiled an even more evil smile—he liked that he was getting to her. "But without water, your pretty little country will die! And when it does, I'll take over the Queendom of Claire and change that frilly, silly little name to the **Kingdom** of **Ooztralia!**"

Queen Bea's gasp, or so the legends all say, lasted almost the rest of that day.

She slowly, menacingly rose from her throne. "As queen of the fair Queendom of Claire—which is my valued and hallowed ancestral home—let it hereby forever be known that I will never reach any agreement with this musty, untrusty, disgusting thing!"

Ooz ran across the room and pulled his ax from the door. "Ah, Your Majesty, be careful what you say before you've thought things thoroughly through," the little man cautioned her. "Will you say the same thing in one week's time—when your lovely green country is gasping for water? I will return for your answer one week from this day."

Then, laughing like the evil ogre he was, Ooz whirled to his right. And left.

"Oh no! What are we going to do?" one of the older elders whispered. "We've got to stop him."

"Not just once," the queen growled. "We must stop him twice!"

"Twice?"

Queen Beatrix held up a finger. "Once, by unblocking the river." Then she held up a second finger. "And twice, by stopping Grak from eating the rest of our trees."

"Oh dear, where does one even begin?" said one of the elders, turning nervously to Queen Bea.

"With the water!" the queen said without hesitation. "We can already see signs of our lake losing water. That cannot happen—Claire must have water. And our army should, hopefully, be able to hold Grak at bay. Well, for now anyway."

"But how can we move all those boulders that are blocking the river?" an elder wondered out loud. "Grak is the only one big enough to do it."

"And even if we could," cried another, "surely that dino could just put them back again!"

"Perhaps we could dig down to find water," someone suggested more helpfully.

"I'm afraid not," Sir Duncan sighed sadly. "There's nothing below us but rock."

"Then perhaps we can find water over there. Or over there. Or there. Or there or there or there," one of the other elders said, turning almost completely around.

"I'm afraid not," Sir Duncan sighed sadly again. "All of Claire's water comes from the River Claire over there— which, as you know, runs through the Sadlands before it gets here. And that's the only water there is."

"Gentlemen, there's only one thing we can do," the queen interrupted. "We must go up."

"Up?" the elders all echoed, completely confused.

"Yes. Look up. Do you see all those clouds everywhere up there in the sky?" She paused while everyone looked. "Well, fortunately for us, they're not made from tufts of fluffy cotton, as they seem. Instead, they are made from..."

She looked expectantly around the Great Hall.

"Water!" someone exclaimed—and everyone immediately jumped up and down with sudden thundering joy.

"Quite right," the queen smiled with a modest bow. "We simply run a pipeline from Lookout Rock up into the clouds and get our water from there until we can find a way to unblock the river."

"Ahhhhh..." The wise men all ahhhhhed at the queen's brilliant suggestion.

Immediately, Sir Duncan brightened as well. "A most brilliant idea, Your Majesty! It seems you have, yet again, saved the Queendom of Claire. I shall have the royal engineers begin work on the pipeline this very day! However"—and he paused—"there's just one other problem."

The queen stiffened. "Yes, I know. That doesn't solve the problem of Grak."

"And his unending appetite for trees," one of the elders added.

Sir Duncan nodded. "Yes. We must find something else for Grak to eat instead of our trees. And we must find it fast! Or soon, there will be nothing for the water from our pipeline to water."

4 Falling from the Sky

Still clinging desperately to slithery fistfuls of weeds, reeds, and rushes, Sir Seth and Sir Ollie found themselves tumbling totally out of control, head over heels in the dark—like clothes in a dryer—with absolutely no idea of what had just happened. Or where they were going. The only thing the two tumbling knights knew for sure was that they had just been GUH-LUMPHED by an enormous tunnel-like pipe that seemed to drop straight down from the bottom of Puddlewater Pond! Which didn't make sense.

However, thanks to the Emergency Escape Course they had taken at the Mighty Knights Knight School, Sir Seth and Sir Ollie instinctively knew exactly what to do. They calmly and coolly cupped their hands around their mouths and bellowed HELP! HELP! at the absolute uppermost tops of their lungs, just in case there was someone nearby.

But all they heard was a distant echo-y: "Woof! Woof!"

"Sir Ollie!" shouted a well-spun Sir Seth. "Do you hear…Shasta?"

Before Sir Ollie could rightly answer, the two Mighty Knights suddenly burst from inside the long, dark pipeline into a double-dazzling splash of yellow sunlight…and in midair, high above a breathtakingly shimmering lake!

Sir Seth and Sir Ollie continued turning in the air as they fell and could now see where they had just come from—it was an open pipe in the sky! Just then, in front of their wide-open eyes, out burst a large wooden raft...with Shasta barely clinging to the rigging with her teeth.

"Sir Ollie, it's the *Mighty Voyager*! And Shasta, too!" Sir Seth shouted to his fast-falling friend. "And they're both comin' right at us!"

"The raft is still attached to our UBHs," cried an amazed Sir Ollie. "What d'we do?"

"Use your UBH to pull yourself on board," cried Sir Seth, following his own instructions. "Quick! We've gotta take the raft's sail and make it into a parachute!"

"Gotcha!" Sir Ollie understood at once.

Without one more word and still dropping like a rock, Sir Ollie quickly clambered onto the raft—past a busily barking and jumping-up-and-down Shasta—and grabbed two corner ropes of the frantically flapping sail, then jumped onto one of the bikes and tied the two corner ropes to the handlebars. Sir Seth

climbed up and over the other side, clawed his way
to the second bike, and untied the ropes holding the sail
to the mast. And tied the ropes to the other handlebars.

The sail instantly snapped into an upside-down letter
"U," and at once, the *Mighty Voyager* began to sail once
again, this time on a cushion of air.

And not a moment too soon.

Because just then, the *Mighty Voyager* landed with
a mighty splash in the warm waiting arms of peaceful
Lake Claire.

For the next few minutes, Sir Ollie and Sir Seth and
Shasta just sat and stared at one another, still too shocked
to talk, and still looking straight up at the pipe in the sky.

Then, when they realized they were actually alive, they began talking at a hundred miles a minute, all at once.

"Wow, making that sail was one of your all-time best ideas!" blurted Sir Ollie. "I thought we were done."

"So did I," said Sir Seth, clinging tightly to a shivering Shasta. "But where are we?"

"And...what happened to Puddlewater Pond?"

"I don't know, but it sure is beautiful, isn't it?" replied Sir Seth as the raft drifted on the easy, lazy breeze.

"Hey, look at that," Sir Ollie gasped, beginning to perk up. "There's a castle over there! Made of glistening marble. How cool is that?"

Sir Seth turned to see what his friend was pointing at. And there it was, in all its glory—the magnificent marbled Castle Claire, glistening like a jewel in the soft morning light. With bright blue-and-gold pennants stirring slightly in the gently blowing breeze atop each of the tall windowed turrets. It was, truly, the most magnificent, royalest, and castley castle any of them had ever seen.

But Sir Ollie was still a little too jittery to get excited just yet. He looked up at Sir Seth. "Hey, seriously, now that we're here—where do you think we are?"

Sir Seth was still busily looking around in open-mouthed awe. "I seriously wish I knew," he had to admit. "Wherever it is, I get the feeling we're a long, long way from home."

Sir Ollie didn't answer right away, then finally said, "Yeah. Me, too."

"And," continued Sir Seth with a wince, "I don't know if this wherever-we-are place is somewhere that Edith-Anne and those Thatchwychian reinforcements are going to be able to find." He looked at his friend. "I think we're really on our own."

This made Sir Ollie a little more uneasy. "Uh, don't forget...I have to be home before the streetlights go on."

"Yeah? Well, I don't see a lot of streetlights at the castle." Sir Seth smiled. "Do you?"

"Nope," Sir Ollie agreed with a grin.

"So I guess that means you get to stay up all night."

"Or until the castle runs out of banana cream pies!" Sir Ollie added, beginning to feel much better. The mention of food always had that calming effect on him.

Slowly but surely, the *Mighty Voyager* drifted toward the long wooden landing at the foot of the pathway up to the magnificent castle. And standing there, waiting to greet them, was a white-haired elder dressed in a long white robe, holding a ceremonial scepter, surrounded by throngs of silent, wide-eyed underlanders of Claire.

"Welcome, my friends, to the Queendom of Claire," he said with a bow. "We couldn't help noticing your, um, rather spectacular arrival. Allow me to introduce myself, if I may. I am Sir Duncan, the queen's confidant and adviser. I've been sent here to greet you by Queen Beatrix the Sixth. You see, you are the first visitors who have ever come here to Claire."

"How do you do, sir," Sir Seth said, returning his bow.

"I'm Sir Seth Thistlethwaite of the errant Mighty Knights of Right & Honor. This is my friend, and also a Mighty Knight, Sir Ollie Everghettz. And here we have my faithful steed, Shasta."

"A pleasure indeed to meet you, Sir Knights," the adviser politely replied. "Perhaps we should make our way to the castle? Queen Beatrix the Sixth is most eager to meet you and discuss what brings you to us."

"You say this place is called Claire?" Sir Ollie asked, as they all began walking up the long winding hill to the castle. "Where's that?"

Sir Duncan looked at him, his wise old eyes suddenly filled with surprise. "You call yourself a knight errant, sir, and you do not know where you are?"

"Um, not really," Sir Ollie had to admit, a bit embarrassed. "We didn't know there was a whole country down here. I didn't think there was anything down here but dirt."

Sir Duncan stopped in his tracks. "Down here? I'm not sure I understand what you mean by 'down here.'"

"Down here in Claire," Sir Seth tried unsuccessfully to explain.

The suspicion in Sir Duncan's eyes grew even greater. "Before we go farther, perhaps you should explain just who you are, sir, and where you are from, as well as your reasons for coming to Claire."

Sir Seth knew he had to think of something fast. But what? Then it came to him in a flash. The scroll that

King Fluster the Fourth sent with Edith-Anne! He frantically fumbled inside his tunic. It was still there, and although the scroll was wet, it was still very readable. SECRET. URGENT. FOR MIGHTY KNIGHTS ONLY.

"Sir Duncan, we bring you this message from our king to your queen," Sir Seth said, bending the truth just a teeny, weeny little bit, the way Mighty Knights are sometimes allowed to do when they can't think of anything else to say. "I can't tell you any more until we are safely inside the castle—if you know what I mean."

"Ahhhhh, yes, yes," the adviser said with a knowing smile. "It's a secret message. I understand perfectly, Sir Knight."

He reached out and pulled on a long golden cord, and immediately a very large guard holding a very long spear appeared at the gate.

"Open the gate!" he commanded. "The Otherlanders are here for an important conference with the queen."

The enormous golden gate clinked and clanked as it creaked opened.

"Hey, Sir Ollie," Sir Seth whispered as they entered the lush, magnificent gardens surrounding the castle. "He called us 'Otherlanders.' I sorta like the sound of that."

But Sir Ollie, the other Otherlander, was in much too much awe of their totally awesome surroundings to hear what his friend had just said. "Wow, this is what a castle should look like," Sir Ollie sighed, gaping at all the glorious grandeur in every direction all around him.

And while the Mighty Knights were busily gushing and gaping and gawking, Sir Duncan led them all the way up to—and into—the Great Hall inside the castle, right to the queen. "Your Majesty, the Otherlanders are here to see you," Sir Duncan announced with a bow.

"Otherlanders, you say?" Queen Beatrix smiled warmly—but somewhat warily—as she stood up, taking each Otherlander by the hand. And the paw. "And just what 'other' land are you from, my good sir knight?"

"Well, um, we're from—" Sir Seth started to say before being suddenly interrupted by a sudden, spectacular...

KUH-PLOSH!

At exactly 10:22 in the morning on that momentous day, the Mighty Knights met Princess Sundra Neeth for the very first time when a large bag of water suddenly arrived from somewhere above and landed squarely on top of Sir Seth's unsuspecting head.

Queen Beatrix immediately jumped to her feet, fuming and booming and extremely upset. "Sundra Neeth! Come down here at once!"

And from somewhere high overhead, a little lady-like voice

drifted down like a tinkling bell. "In a minute, Mother. Just as soon as I finish reloading."

"Guards! Guards!" Queen Beatrix boomed a little bit louder. "Get up there and find her this instant! And tell her to stop wasting our water!"

But of course, by the time the guards got all the way up to the windowed dome high above the Great Hall, the princess was already on her way down to the kitchen.

"I am so sorry," the queen said, turning bright red but calming down slightly. "The princess will join us shortly." She leaned closer to the two knights. "Now then, you were about to tell me where you are from, and why you have come."

Sir Seth looked at Sir Ollie. And Sir Ollie looked at Sir Seth. Neither knight knew where to begin.

"Um...well, we're sorta from Thatchwych, y'might say," Sir Ollie began.

"Sorta from Thatchwych?" The queen's round hazel eyes shrunk down to slits. "No one is 'sorta' from anywhere, Sir Knight! Everyone is precisely from somewhere. Let me repeat, sir: where precisely are you from?"

"Well, um, we're from up there," Sir Ollie stuttered, pointing to the high atrium overhead.

"Up there? Up where?" the queen repeated. "From the roof of the castle?"

Sir Ollie looked to his friend for help. "Um, did you know there's another country up there, above Claire?"

The queen was amused. "Another country, you say? Floating around somewhere up there in the air?"

"Yes," Sir Seth said seriously. "It's on the other side of those clouds."

Now the queen was totally amused. "Don't be so silly. Clouds don't have other sides. They're one of the few things that don't—the same as ideas and wishes and wind. Clouds simply extend from here all the way up to the Beyond—where they stop."

Now it was the two knights' turn to be surprised. "The Beyond?"

"Yes. The Beyond. That's where the sky ends," she explained, with the wave of one hand. "Everyone knows that!"

Sir Seth looked up into her eyes. "Well, then, have you ever wondered what's on the other side of the Beyond?"

Queen Beatrix looked down at them. "Yes, of course. There's nothing but more and more Beyond beyond that. It just goes and goes until you can't go any farther."

"What's the Beyond got to do with what's down here?" Sir Ollie finally asked.

"Um, Your Majesty," Sir Duncan interrupted, "perhaps we could finish this conversation some other time?"

"Yes, Sir Duncan, I agree," the queen said as she brought a hand to her chin. "So, Sir Seth and Sir Ollie, you are knights errant? Meaning you travel near and far to fight for justice and right and to help the downtrodden. Is that right?"

"That's us," piped up Sir Ollie.

"You can count on Sir Ollie and me, Your Majesty," Sir Seth stated. "What is your problem?"

"Gentlemen," the queen said as she rose from her throne, "it seems that Claire finds itself in a bit of a fix—and we desperately need the help of two gallant crusaders such as yourselves."

She then went on at great length to explain the entire tangled tale of Ooz's evil actions, and when she was finished, she sat and stared deep into the eyes of the young knights. "As you can quite plainly see, your timely arrival in the Queendom of Claire—from whatever land you claim to be from—may be most fortunate, after all. If we could persuade you to help us solve our little water shortage with the evil Mister Ooz, then you will have proven your worth to us all—as well as the truth behind your words. Will you help us?"

Wordlessly, Sir Seth turned to Sir Ollie and drew his sword.

"A Mighty Knight will do whatever he must..."

Sir Ollie also drew El Gonzo and formed the letter X with Sir Seth. "...to take a wrong and make it a right!"

"All we need to know now is where Ooz and Grak live," they both stated.

"I can show you the way," a young girl's voice suddenly said from somewhere behind them.

"Sundra Neeth, you'll do no such thing," the queen bellowed again. "Go to your room!"

"Mother, please!" the princess sniffed in a snit. "Let me go with them. I'm so bored with this dumb old castle I could scream."

Sir Duncan protectively enfolded her in his arms. "No, my princess. Not only do you not know where they're headed, but the country out there beyond the castle is much too dangerous a place for a princess to be, I'm afraid. And where they're going is a place to which you don't know the way. Because, you see, this assignment will take Sir Seth and Sir Ollie deep into the dreaded Sadlands!"

She looked up at him, more wide-eyed than usual. "The what?"

Princess Sundra noticed that the old man's hands were actually shaking.

"The Sadlands. No one wants go there. It's the dreariest, eeriest, most frightening place you can imagine. Just mile after mile of foot-frying, sunburnt sand. Even the vultures avoid it whenever they can. It's so hot in the Sadlands, I once saw a Fibb fry an egg on an ice cube.

No, no, my princess, you don't want to go there. There's nothing but sand, sand, and more sand—then more and more sand after that—all the way to the Beyond."

"But I want some adventure!" the princess cried. "Let me find that Ooz. I could teach him a lesson on…"

"No, no, no," said Sir Duncan hastily. "Let's you and I go for a lovely walk in the gardens instead, hmm?"

"I'm so sick of those boring old gardens I could scream!" As so, the princess did indeed scream, and then ran from the room.

"Well, Sir Ollie, looks like it's just you and me."

Sir Ollie was still thinking about what Sir Duncan had said. "Yeah, but…"

Sir Seth turned to his friend. "But?"

"Well, I thought maybe we should get some sunscreen, that's all."

Sir Duncan walked the two knights to the window and put a hand on their shoulders. The three of them stood there staring down at the endless sun-bleached desert together. "Go carefully, my fine, fearless friends. Adventure aplenty awaits you out there. But danger abounds there as well."

Pho Phum the Fibb looked
down from his perch high atop
bleak, sun-bleached Condor Canyon.

"Well, now, jes lookit this, would yuh?
Them little knights 'ave come back wit' their
dog." He smiled a wily grin, stroking his pointy,
scraggily chin.

Pho is a dust-blown desert dweller who happened
to be unwittingly sitting on top of Lookout Rock
at the precise moment the Mighty Knights burst
through the pipe in the sky in their surprise power
dive. That's him there, squatting in the middle.
His fearsome son with the squinty eyes, Phee, is on
the right, and beside him, on the left, is Pho Phum's
fair daughter, Phi, with the sneaky little eyes. They
are Fibbs—wily, smiley little sand travelers, who live

by their wits and on the cactus soup and sandwiches they're somehow able to find somewhere out there in the unending sand. Well, at least that's what they say, anyway—because it's almost impossible to tell whether a Fibb's fibbing or telling the truth. Or to understand anything it's saying at all.

Phee Phum leaned forward. "Want me t' call t' condors wit' me whistle, Father?"

Phee was referring to the pet King Claire condors that the Phums use to get to wherever they're going. They're also fairly useful for frightening off Phum family foes with their long pointed beaks and fearsome talons. Although, as birds go, these condors are quite big, it also follows that Fibbs must, by comparison, be somewhat small if they are to ride on a condor at all. Fortunately, Phee, Phi, and Pho are just three feet tall—the perfect size to ride upon the nasty King Claire condors they love so much.

"Yup," his father agreed. "We bes' git ourselves down there and find out whut these fellahs want."

Phee Phum turned and screeched like a condor, and in less than four seconds flat, the Phum family condors were saddled and standing beside them.

"Ready t'go, Father," Phee said, stroking Pho's bird on the nose.

Pho Phum hopped on his bird's back and tapped its ribs with his toes. At once, the big bird opened its wings wide and soared majestically out over the canyon.

Meanwhile, way down below, on the sunbaked desert floor in the absolute middle of nowhere at all, Sir Seth caught the sudden overhead motion in the corner of his eye.

"Uh-oh."

"Uh, why did you just say 'uh-oh'?" Sir Ollie wanted to know, shielding his eyes from the sun. "What're you 'uh-ohing' about?"

"Well, y'know, I was sorta wondering about something."

"About what?"

"Do, um, condors eat knights?"

"Uh-oh," Sir Ollie agreed when he saw the big birds circling high overhead. "I don't know what condors eat, but let's make sure we're not on the menu. C'mon, quick! Let's hide behind those big boulders over there."

Without thinking, the three Mighty Knights ran and dove behind the huge rocks—and landed face first in the sticky, gooey mess of a dune bug's candy-floss web. In case you've never seen a dune bug before, it's about the same size as that fat cat over there, except it's not quite that color—or nearly as wide—and has seven legs all on one side. Which explains why a dune bug never leaves its home. With seven legs all on the same side, it's usually too busy walking around in circles to wander anywhere that far away.

"Ohhhhh no!" the dune bug lamented loudly, looking at what was left of her web. "Didn't your mother ever tell you to look before you leap? Now I'll have to start all over again. And it's 112 degrees in the shade."

Sir Seth smiled lamely, jumping back as best he could, still tangled in the long, sticky strands of pink candy floss. "Sorry about that. We didn't know you were here."

"Well, now that you know, you may as well stay here, where you'll be safe," she sighed. "Not even a Fibb as foolish as Pho would fly into a gooey mess of molasses on a day as hot as this," she said. "So, anyway, how do you do? My name is June Bugg, the dune bug."

"Uh…a Fibb?" asked Sir Seth.

"Yeah," the dune bug replied. "That's them flying around on those condors up there."

"Oh. Well, I'm Sir Seth Thistlethwaite. And these are—"

"Yes, yes, I already know that," June smiled.

"You do?" Sir Seth said with surprise. "How come?"

June's smile grew even larger.

"The news of your arrival is all over the Hot Rock Hotline," she said, pulling a long candy-floss strand from the back of Sir Seth's hand. "Everyone in Claire knows that you're here, and where you're going."

"What's the Hot Rock Hotline?" Sir Seth wondered out loud.

"Gossip! Nothing but gossip all day long," June said. "Out here, all the rocks can talk. So they just sit around and babble all day—because there's nothing else for them to do. But today, even they don't know what's happened to Princess Sundra Neeth."

"The princess?" Sir Ollie joined the conversation. "She's still at the castle. She wanted to come with us, but her mother said no."

June said, rather nervously now, "But the word on the hotline only a moment ago was that Princess Sundra Neeth is not at the castle."

"Uh-oh. Where did she go?" Sir Seth wondered out loud.

"Nobody knows," June sighed.

"I bet I know!" Sir Ollie said, still wrapped up in floss. "I'll bet she's gone to take on Ooz all by herself!"

"By golly, Sir Ollie, you're probably right!" Sir Seth said. He looked up at the condors circling overhead.

"And I bet that flying's the best way to find her."

"Flying!" Sir Ollie groaned, pulling off more of the long, stubborn strands of sticky candy floss. "I can't even walk until we ungoo and unglue ourselves from this mess. I sure wish there was some water around here."

"So does everyone else." June smiled dryly. "But the only water anywhere around here is down there in the River Claire—and that's been blocked off by all those rocks."

Before anyone could say anything more, the three huge condors swept down and lightly alit next to where Shasta was wagging and eating her way out of the toe-tangling candy-floss web.

Pho Phum dropped down from his mighty mount and stood there staring at the two knights with his narrow slitty eyes, while Phee and Phi Phum began to walk over to Sir Seth and Sir Ollie.

"Hi," Sir Ollie finally greeted them. "Be with you in a minute..."

"No need t'urry," the little man grunted and sat down.

Without a word, Phee Phum reached down and grasped one of the long strands of floss that was wound around and around one of Sir Ollie's arms.

"Lie down" is all he said.

Sir Ollie wasn't sure what Phee wanted, but he sensed it might be a good idea not to tell the Fibbs too much about anything yet—because they're probably called Fibbs for a very good reason.

Quickly, Phee and Phi began scooping handfuls of sand all over Sir Seth and Shasta, until they, too, were covered in toasty yellow-brown sand from their heads to their toes.

"Okay, she be unstuck," Phi said to Phee. "Ready? Go!"

He held on to that one strand of floss with both hands, while Phi began rolling Sir Ollie over and over across the sand, unraveling the long single string of sandy candy floss. And when she was finished, Sir Ollie was completely unstuck, ungooed, and unglued, and stood up as clean as a whistle.

"Ahhhhh-mazing," he gasped. "Thank you."

But Phee and Phi were too busy ungluing Sir Seth and Shasta to hear what Sir Ollie said. And still Pho Phum just sat there, staring.

"Now..." Pho finally said, taking a handful of sand and making a little pyramid in front of him.

"Now?" wondered a freshly freed Sir Seth, who sat down across from the strange little man. "Now what?"

Pho Phum didn't look up. "Well, I gots two t'ings I'd like t'ask yuh. Who are yuh? And whut d'yuh want?"

Sir Seth looked at Sir Ollie. Then—deciding that freeing the knights from the dune bug's wily web made the Fibbs worthy of their trust—Sir Seth took a deep breath. He did his best to explain everything he knew about the hole in the bottom of Puddlewater Pond, only the more he tried to explain, the more unbelievable everything sounded.

"So...there's a pond o'water up in them clouds is there?" scoffed Pho. "Ha! Y'sound more like a Fibb than me!"

Sir Seth was just about to try another way of telling the story when, from out of nowhere, a fiery arrow streaked across the afternoon sky and buried itself in the sand at Pho Phum's feet. Everyone was too shocked to move. Then Sir Ollie noticed...

"Look! There's a note."

Phee Phum grabbed the note before it could burn.

"Whut d'she say?" Phi wanted to know, looking over Phee's shoulder.

He looked nervously at his father. "All she sez is... 'Go Home!'"

"Humph," Pho Phum grumped. And that was all.

"Who's it from?" Phi asked.

"Ooz! Who else?" Pho Phum grumped again.

"Whut d'yuh think we should we do?" Phi wanted to know.

"It sez 'Go Home,' so let's go home," Phee suggested.

Phi looked around. "But I already am home."

"Maybe he means Lookout Rock," Phee tried again. "That's home, too."

"Wherever a Fibb finds his feet is home," Pho said firmly.

"Y'know, Father," suggested Phi, "maybe if we jes tried talkin' t'Ooz 'bout..."

"No! No! No way!" Pho whirled fiercely, with menace in every word. "Ooz 'as gotta learn that t'Sadlands is our land, too. Not jes 'is. D'yuh unnerstand?"

Then Pho turned to the Mighty Knights with his slitty little eyes and hissed, "Now fer once and fer all...jes who are yuh? And whose side are y'on?"

Sir Seth took yet another deep breath and went to try answering again, but Sir Ollie stepped in instead. "We're the Mighty Knights of Right & Honor," he said, "and Queen Beatrix the Sixth has asked us to help her."

"'Elp 'er?" Pho grunted. "T'do whut?"

It was Sir Ollie's turn to take a deep breath. "She has asked us to drive Ooz out of the Queendom of Claire and forever rid it of that evil, awful elf!"

"And that goes for his buddy Grak, too," Sir Seth snorted. "He'll just have to eat somebody else's trees from now on."

Then, right then and right there, for the first time in all of his two hundred and forty-four years, Pho Phum looked up at the knights and smiled a real smile. Not his usual wily smile. But a smiley smile. It was a small smiley smile that really wasn't much of a smile at all. But there was no doubt, it was the first real un-wily smile that Pho Phum had ever smiled—no matter what size it was.

The minute he saw it, Sir Seth thought it would be a good time to ask, "Will you help us?"

Still smiling, Pho Phum sat up and Fibbishly said, "Yup."

But just remember, a Fibb "yup" isn't the same "yup" you'd get from anyone else. A Fibb "yup" is more like a "maybe." Or a "what's in it for me?" And sometimes, a Fibb "yup" even means "nup," which means "no" in anyone else's language. So next time you hear a Fibb say "yup," don't jump to any conclusions.

"Good!" said Sir Seth, standing up, getting ready to go, "Now all we need to know is where Ooz lives."

"He lives in a cave way over there, on t'other side of t'desert, don'tcha know," Phi Phum replied, pointing across miles and miles of yellow searing sand and sun-baked boulders and rock. "But he could be jes 'bout anywheres out there at all." He held up the arrow that was just shot at them.

"Yep, yep," Phee added excitedly. "And Grak only eats peas and trees and knights, don'tcha know."

"Yeah? Well, you can tell Grak that the Mighty Knights only eat peas, trees, and dinos for dinner," Sir Seth declared dashingly, drawing his sword. "Right, Sir Ollie?"

His friend completed the X with El Gonzo, his sword. "Right on, Sir Seth! It's time for the Mighty Knights to ride!"

"Y'bes' be careful where y'go in t'desert," Pho warned them with a wily smile. "B'lieve me, there be lotsa critters and creatures out there yuh don't want t'meet."

"Yeah! Like desert sandragons!" Phee shuddered.

"Sandragons?" Sir Ollie echoed nervously. "What's a sandragon?"

"And saw-toothed knee gnawers!" Phi added.

"Knee gnawers?" Sir Ollie echoed. "Do they really gnaw your knees?"

"And dune daddlers, too, don'tcha know." Pho cringed at the thought.

"Oh no! What does a dune daddler do when it daddles you?" Sir Ollie worriedly wondered as he began seeing this assignment in an entirely nervous new light. "And... and...uh, there's another problem, too," he said, turning to Pho. "That's a long way to walk on a day as double-deadly hot as this."

Pho Phum thought about it for a moment. "Well, there be too many of us t'ride on t'condors together..." Then his beady little eyes lit up. He turned to Phee. "Do them umbies still live out there by Knock-Knock Rock?"

"Yup," Phee confirmed.

"Good," he said, then turned to Sir Seth and Sir Ollie. "Maybe we should all jes git over t'Knock-Knock Rock fer a chat."

"How do we do that?"

Pho smiled that little smile of his again. "Oh, Knock-Knock ain't far t'walk. She be jes over t'next dune over there. And we can find y'some umbies t'ride, fer sure."

Sir Seth excitedly turned to Sir Ollie. "Okay, then. Knock-Knock Rock, it is. Let's go!"

6 Into the Sadlands

Sir Ollie turned to Pho Phum and slumped down in the sand with a thump. "You said Knock-Knock Rock was just beyond the next dune."

"Yup," Pho Phum agreed with a grin. "That's whut I said."

"Well, that was about three dunes ago, and we're still not there yet."

"Oh, whut I meant t'say wuz it's t'dune that's after t'one that's after t'dune after that," Pho explained, without explaining all that much. "Which means it's t'dune we're comin' t' next."

"Oh, okay," Sir Ollie said, still confused. "Um...so tell me, what does an umbie look like anyhow?"

Which was quite a good question, if you've never seen an umbie before. Umbies look a lot like ostriches, except they're not quite so cute. They're sort of gawky and balky with a wobbly, knobbly tangle of legs—and large lacy wings shaped like umbrellas. You'll often find some clustered in flocks around Knock-Knock Rock, where they take turns shading themselves by standing on each other's heads and flapping their wings. Which means there are two kinds of umbies—over-umbies and under-umbies. The under-umbies, of course, are the ones on the bottom, and the over-umbies are the umbies on top—until the under-umbies on the bottom swap with the over-umbies on top. Which makes all the over-umbies under-umbies again.

Somewhere in middle of Pho's explaining this to Sir Seth and Sir Ollie, they finally did arrive among a band of umbies at Knock-Knock Rock. Pho was about to begin talking to one of the umbies when Knock-Knock Rock rudely interrupted.

"Um, excuse me, but aren't you forgetting something?" the rock said, stone-faced and unsmiling.

Pho cocked his head. "Me? Ferget somethin'? Like whut?"

The rock sniffed, rather miffed. "Surely you know by now you can't just walk up and talk to an umbie without telling me a knock-knock joke first. That's why I'm called Knock-Knock Rock. Remember?"

"Oh, uh, sorry." Pho Phum sort of blushed beneath all the dust. "Okay...ready? Knock, knock."

"Who's there?"

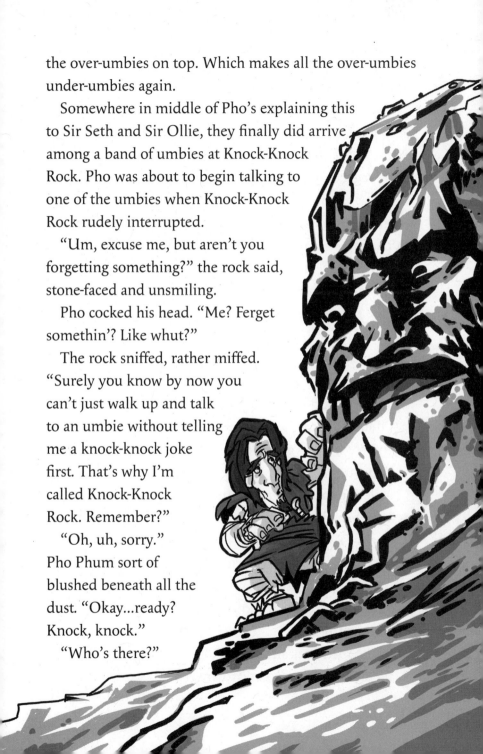

"Wanda."

"Wanda who?

"Wanda 'elp find us some umbies?"

"Oh, ho, ho! That was a good one," the rock snickered. "Now you can go over there and talk to the umbies."

The raggedy group wasted no time. Pho turned to Sir Seth and Sir Ollie. "Git on over there and pick out an umbie—quick! Phi, you go wit' 'em and 'elp. I'll be wit'cha in a minnit."

"Who, me?" Phi Phum suddenly looked nervous, before calming herself down. "It's jes that...well, Father, maybe I should go up and, uh, be yer eyes in t'sky! Keep a lookout! If yer stayin' down there in t'desert wit' t'knights and all."

Pho cocked his head for a moment, then agreed. "Yup, yup, good idea. Up y'go."

"I'll help 'em with t'umbies, Father," Phee Phum volunteered. "You go make a deal wit 'em."

"Yup, yup, off y'go," Pho agreed again.

While the gallant band of knights went over to pick out their umbies, Pho Phum hurried over to the lead umbie.

"Hi, I'm Pho Phum, the Fibb," he said, "and I 'ave three friends whut needs a ride. How much willit cost?"

"A ride?" the umbie grumped, eyeing the little man suspiciously with its sad hound-dog eyes. "I don't do business with Fibbs."

Pho stepped back in shock. "Oh? And why not?"

The big bird leaned forward angrily. "Because the last

time I did business with a Fibb, the Fibb didn't pay me!"

Pho quickly rummaged around in the sack he was wearing over one shoulder and pulled out a tattered old cactus sandwich. "I can pay yuh. See? And there be lots more o' that where this comes from."

The umbie suddenly broke into a great big trusting grin. "Excellent! Well now, how can I help you?" the umbie wanted to know.

Meanwhile, as he waited for his ride, Sir Ollie found himself worriedly watching the shifting, drifting sand off to his right as it slowly formed itself into what appeared to be a ten-foot-long alligator slithering toward them.

"Uh, guys, there's a..." he started to warn everyone, but then the menacing shape just disappeared back under the sand.

"I need t'take three friends cross t'desert," Pho said, putting the battered sandwich back in his sack.

Pho Phum had no intention of paying the umbie at all. But just by talking about payment, Pho created the impression that the umbie would be getting paid. So you can see how a Fibb like Pho Phum can tell a fib without telling a lie.

The umbie thought about it briefly. "Well, let me see now. That'll be three soup-and-sandwiches a day, for each of the six of us—all the way there and all the way back."

Pho looked the umbie in the eye. "Six umbies?"

"Yes. You need three under-umbies to carry each of your friends, and three over-umbies to sit on top of

the three under-umbies' heads to shade them," the big
bird replied. "You can't cross the Sadlands without any
shade. And the only shade around here is on those under-
umbies over there with the over-umbies on their backs."

"Yuh drive a 'ard bargain," Pho sighed, "but let's go."

Sir Ollie had quickly hopped onboard his under-
umbie—and was waiting for his over-umbie to arrive—
when, once again, off to his right, the mysterious sand-
blown shape reappeared. Now it was about twenty feet
long, but whatever was making it was still out of sight
under the sand. But before he could say anything, Pho
Phum waddled over to Sir Seth.

"Shove over, young fellah. I'll ride up there wit'cha fer
a while. We can talk."

Sir Seth looked down at Pho Phum as an over-umbie
hopped up onto the clumsy under-umbie's head. "Um,
shouldn't we take some water with us?"

"Yeah," Sir Ollie agreed, looking out across the blazing
expanse of shimmering sand. "That's a looooong way to
go without any water."

"No problem," Pho shrugged. "We'll fill up on t'first
chuggamugga bug we meet."

"The first what?" Sir Ollie asked.

"Chuggamugga bug. They're everywhere out here,"
Pho Phum said. "They be so fulla water, a chuggamugga
bug's like a mug o' water wit' legs. But c'mon, we gotta
git goin'."

"I'm ready, but how do you get these umbies to go?"

Sir Seth asked, picking up the reins on his under-umbie.

"Y'jes tap 'em in t'ribs wit' yer toes."

Which Sir Seth did. And immediately, the big bird lurched unsteadily and began to walk like a camel.

Pho looked up at Sir Seth with his slitty little eyes. "So tell me somethin', Mister Knight: jes how're yuh plannin' on gettin' rid of Ooz and his tree-eatin' friend?"

Sir Seth looked into the little man's beady blue eyes. "Well, I thought we'd—"

"Uh, guys, there's, there's, there's a..." Sir Ollie tried to warn them once again.

But the Fibb interrupted him and pushed aside a clump of dusty, tangled curls. "Well, I surely do hope y'can do it," he sighed sadly. "I surely do. A long time ago, t'Fibbs tried and tried to get Ooz t'go somewheres else...and now there be but three of us left."

"What happened to the other Fibbs?" Sir Seth gasped.

"I guess most of 'em jes up and left fer somewheres nicer'n this, where there be grasslands and trees...like all this once used t' be." Pho sighed even more sadly. "As for t'rest? I really don't know." Then he looked at Sir Seth and laughed. "Maybe Grak ate t'entire family tree. Whut d'yuh think?"

"That dino really ate all the trees and the grass?" Sir Seth asked.

Pho Phum sighed. "Ooz cut 'em down and Grak ate 'em. And wit'out any shade, the sun fried all t'roots of t'grass and turned everything into a desert."

"All the trees?" Sir Seth repeated in complete disbelief.

"Yup. Well, most of 'em, anyhow. Grak is mighty big, don'tcha know. He's even bigger'n dis," Pho said, spreading his arms as wide as they would go. "He's big as Castle Claire, wit' an appetite about t'same size. They say he can down a small forest all in one sittin' when he gets hungry enough, and I b'lieve 'em."

"Oh yeah?" Sir Ollie finally managed to shout at the top of his voice. "Well, right now, there's a sand alligator even bigger than that that's about to eat US!"

"An alligator?" Sir Seth shouted across to his friend.

"There aren't any alligators in the middle of a desert."

"No?! Well, what do you call that?"

Everyone saw it at the same time—the unmistakable shape of a for-real...

"SANDRAGON!!"

Pho Phum roared.

"Oh no! Everyone, *RUN!!*"

Right on cue, an eeeeenormous snarling, fire-breathing
sandragon erupted from under the sand a mere thirty-
two or -three feet away and reared up on its hind legs,
blasting blinding furnace-like blasts of bright yellow fire
in every direction. Which fricasseed all the feathers on
each and every umbie, and immediately started a frantic
over- and under-umbie stampede.

However, when umbies stampede, they don't run
away. For some reason, they run toward one another
instead.

So the moment the fire-breathing dragon appeared, all
the umbies began screeching and squawking and swirling
and whirling and running in ever-diminishing circles,
until all that was left was a tall, trembling tower
of terrified umbies sitting on top of each other's heads.
And somewhere in the middle of all that tangle of
knobbly knees, the Mighty Knights, Pho and Phee Phum,
and Shasta were desperately trying to get free.

And all the while, the ferocious fire-breathing
sandragon stood there menancingly, catching its
breath for another frightfully flame-filled blast of hot
yellow fire.

Ooz Prepares a Surprise

7

Just outside Ooz's dark, dreary cave, Grak was
busily fussing over the steaming stewpot on the
huge crackling fire, preparing his favorite recipe:
Chopped Knight Delight. He dipped a long claw into the
pot and sampled the simmering broth boiling inside.

"Ah, just about right," he rumbled with a voice deeper
than rolling thunder. "But it needs perhaps a peck of pea
pods and a dash of smoked oak," he purred with utter
delight, taking another long, savory sip. "Mmmmm,
and another cord of that woodsy walnut wouldn't hurt.
Plus a nippy splash of ash, along with a sprinkle of sassy
sassafras leaf to flesh out the flavor." Then he suddenly
frowned. "Of course what my Chopped Knight Delight
really needs is...a sprig of nice spicy knight."

Ooz trundled over to the enormous fire and sat down.
He finished sharpening his ax on a well-worn rock and
very carefully ran one thumb along the glistening edge.

"Well, Grak, my famished old friend, I have some
rather exciting news to brighten your otherwise drab,
dreary day!"

Grak looked down from what he was doing. "Yeah?"

Ooz whirled and hurled his ax at one of the last
trees still standing anywhere in the Sadlands. "By this
time tomorrow, I promise you, you'll be feasting on
beech, birch, and balsa, and filbert and fir—and fillet of

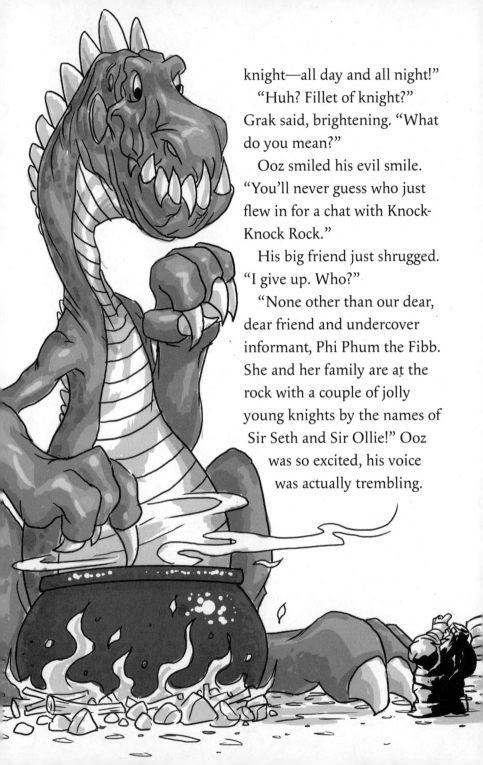

knight—all day and all night!"

"Huh? Fillet of knight?" Grak said, brightening. "What do you mean?"

Ooz smiled his evil smile. "You'll never guess who just flew in for a chat with Knock-Knock Rock."

His big friend just shrugged. "I give up. Who?"

"None other than our dear, dear friend and undercover informant, Phi Phum the Fibb. She and her family are at the rock with a couple of jolly young knights by the names of Sir Seth and Sir Ollie!" Ooz was so excited, his voice was actually trembling.

When he heard the word "knights," Grak suddenly began listening very intently. "Did you say knights? Oh, I haven't had a knight for days and days and days."

"Not just one knight, but two!" Ooz oozed with delight. "And not only that but Phi had some very, very, very interesting information she was willing to share for some, um, shall we say...future considerations."

Grak went back to his stirring. "Yeah? Like what?"

"Are you sitting down? Get ready for this!" Ooz smiled an even eviler smile. "Go ahead—guess what Phi just told me."

"Uhhhhh...I give up."

"It's all over the Hot Rock Hotline. Princess Sundra Neeth, the poor little dear, is wandering around in the fearsome, searing Sadlands—completely and lamentably lost! And utterly alone."

He leaned back smugly, waiting for Grak's excited answer—which didn't come. Which immediately urged Ooz to continue.

"Think about it, Grak. Think what that means!"

"Uhhh, I dunno...what?"

Ooz waved one arm in a sweep. "Just look around you. Tell me what you see."

"Not much. Just desert."

"Right!" Ooz eagerly agreed. "Nothing but sand. And if you could, what would you rather see out there instead?"

"Uh...well, a nice tasty forest of fir would be good.

Or some yummy beech, birch, and balsa and a field full of peas."

"Right!" Ooz enthused, getting even more excited. "And where can we find forests of fir and fields filled with peas?"

Grak didn't have to think long. "Well, there's lots over there. On the other side of the treeline, in the south of Claire."

"Right you are all over again! And if it weren't for that Royal Army of theirs, all of it would be ours! But what if Claire somehow belonged to us?"

"Yeah. If Claire belonged to us."

Ooz stood up on his tiptoes for his grand finale. "Well, Grak, my fine famished friend, I now know how Claire can belong to us!"

Grak gasped so deeply, he almost inhaled Ooz. "You do?"

"Indeed I do," Ooz enthused. "All we have to do is take a little trip down to the desert, just you and me, and 'rescue' precious Princess Sundra Neeth. Now do you see what I mean?"

"Uh, no...what?"

"Think about it, you lumbering, lumber-headed lout! We simply swoop down, scoop up the princess, and bring her back here, where we can hold her for ransom! The Queendom of Claire will be all OURS! Every pea, tree, and knight of it!" Ooz whooped at the top of his voice. "And just for good measure, we'll also 'rescue'

Queen Beatrix's two precious knights, Sir Seth and
Sir Ollie, and bring them back here for ransom as well!"

Grak simply nodded his eager agreement.

Ooz cupped his hand and whispered. "If Queen Beatrix
was shocked when we blocked the river, I can't wait till
she hears about this! Here's how it works:

"ONE. I go to Castle Claire and announce to the
queen that we have 'rescued' her precious Princess
Sundra Neeth.

"TWO. As usual, she starts ranting and raving at the
top of her voice, 'What must I do to get my daughter
back?'

"THREE. Then I calmly say—in my inarguable
winning way—'It's quite easy, Your Majesty. You simply
give me the Queendom of Claire, and in return, Grak
and I will give you your daughter.'

"FOUR. Finally, Queen Beatrix the Sixth signs the
Magna Charter of Claire over to me, which—formally
and officially and beyond any dispute—makes me the
king of the Queendom of Claire! No, wait, how could
I forget? The KINGdom of OOZtralia!!"

He paused grandly, waiting for the standing ovation.
But Grak—whose mind had wandered during Ooz's
rather lengthy speech—just stood there stirring his stew.

"Well? Isn't that just too, too good to be true? In fact,
to make this happy ending even happier still, perhaps
my dear, dear friend and informant, Phi Phum the Fibb,
could even be made my new queen…" At this thought,

Ooz's grin began to grow too large for his face. "Of course, it would be the only way of thanking her for passing along this very, very, very useful information."

"Yeah? What information is that?" Grak said, now far more interested in stirring his pot than in the thought of being a friend of the new King of Claire...or Ooztralia... or whatever it would be called.

Ooz snorted. "Never mind," he shrugged. "I'll try telling you later." He walked over and stood looking out on the desert, sharpening another ax. "I think I know what they mean when they say it's lonely at the top," he said to himself.

Giant Steps

8

Sir Seth Thistlethwaite stood frozen
in fear, gawking up into the wide-open
mouth of the fire-breathing sandragon. Its
mouth was so big and the dragon was so
close, he could even see that little dangly
thing like the one he had at the back of
his throat. He thought it would have
been burned to a crisp a long time ago.
"Quick, quick, run! While he's
gettin' 'is second wind!" Pho
Phum urged the two knights,
pulling them by the arms.
"Them sandragons be

big and scary, but they can't move more'n 'alf a inch a hour."

Sir Ollie looked nervously at Sir Seth. "If that was his first wind, I don't think I want to know what the second one's like."

"I'm with you," Sir Seth heartily agreed. "Let's ride!"

"I've got Shasta," Sir Ollie said. "C'mon, here we go!"

The Mighty Knights and Pho Phum ran as fast as they could in the ankle-deep sand, then they stopped and flopped—and turned around when they thought they were a safe distance from the sandragon's flames.

"Wow, running in this sand is like running in slo-mo," Sir Ollie gasped and knelt down, huffing and puffing. "It's a good thing it took that dragon this long to reload."

"Hmmmm, so it did." Pho Phum scratched his tangled mop. "But it usually don't. I wonder why?"

The big sandragon was still standing there, with wisps of blue smoke seeping out of each nostril and a puzzled look on its face. It seemed to be trying to get something out of its mouth.

"Whoo!" Phee cried from overhead. "Got 'im, Father!"

Everyone looked up. And there was Phee Phum circling on his condor, which he'd called with his trusty condor-calling whistle.

"Now, jes lookit that, would yuh!" Pho said proudly. "Phee loves that there whistle. And he brought t'bucket, too."

"The bucket?" Sir Ollie asked. "What can you do with

a bucket out here in the desert?"

"Phee's gonna show yuh right now," the scruffy little man said, smiling. "Watch this..."

Right on cue, Phee Phum reached forward and tapped his condor on the back of its head, and as soon as he did, the big bird tucked in its wings and nosed over into a screaming dive-bombing run. It dropped like a rock, almost straight down, then at the last second, when it was right above the sandragon, the condor abruptly pulled up—and dumped the entire bucket of sand directly on the dragon's still-smoldering head.

Only this time, the sandragon remembered to keep its big mouth shut.

"Bull's eye!" Sir Ollie whooped, still looking up. "Whoo! Good for you!"

"Yeah, now we know what to do if it happens again." Sir Seth sighed with relief as he slowly got to his feet. "Well, I guess the air show's over—for now, anyhow— but where's Phi? Doesn't she have a bucket, too?" he wondered, also looking up.

Everyone scanned the open sky. But only Phee's condor could be seen.

"Oh, sure she'll be along," Pho finally said, not so certainly. "She be somewheres up there, keepin' an eye on t'ings fer us."

"So now what are we going to do?" Sir Ollie said, staring out across the almost endless desert. "Where did the umbies all go?"

"Oh, that Sandragon musta scared 'em all t'way up t'Gorgon Grotto t'hide."

"Gorgon Grotto? Where's that?"

"Jes beyond t'next dune over there," Pho Phum said with a shrug. "Or maybe it's t'dune after that."

Sir Ollie looked nervously at the little man. "So the umbies are gone and we're all alone? In the middle of the desert?"

"Yup. 'Fraid so." Pho shrugged again.

"Soooo what do we do?" Sir Ollie wondered out loud, still staring out across the vast sunbaked expanse of desert. "That's a long, hot walk without an umbie to shade us."

"I surely wish I knew," Pho Phum sighed unsurely.

"If you want a ride," a voice suddenly said from up high, from somewhere nearby, "I'll be glad to give you one. In fact, I insist!"

The Mighty Knights and Fibbs quickly looked up. Then up and up some more. And there, behind them, was Ooz, the evil, awful elf—with an ax, as usual, clutched in each hand—suspended a hundred skyscraping feet in the air, and perched on top of the head of a rather big dino.

It was Grak!

This overgrown lizard was so way-up-high-in-the-sky big, he made the sandragon seem about as scary as Claireberry pie. In fact, Grak was SOOOOO mega-monstrously big, he even scared the sandragon right back under the sand.

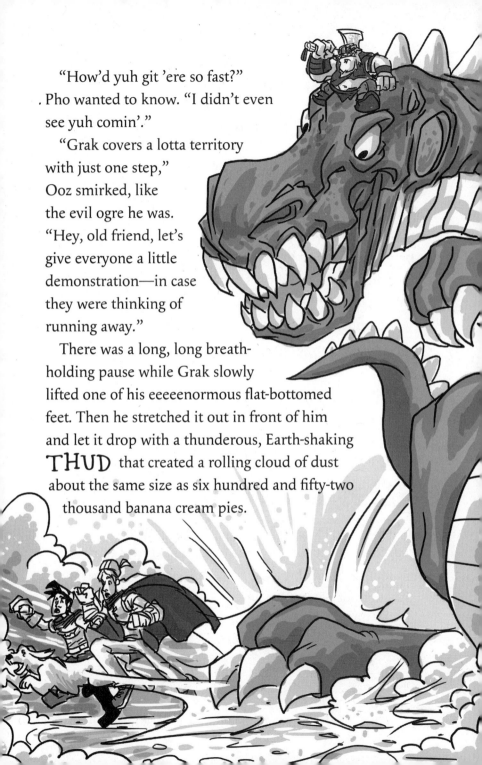

"How'd yuh git 'ere so fast?"
Pho wanted to know. "I didn't even
see yuh comin'."

"Grak covers a lotta territory
with just one step,"
Ooz smirked, like
the evil ogre he was.
"Hey, old friend, let's
give everyone a little
demonstration—in case
they were thinking of
running away."

There was a long, long breath-
holding pause while Grak slowly
lifted one of his eeeeenormous flat-bottomed
feet. Then he stretched it out in front of him
and let it drop with a thunderous, Earth-shaking
THUD that created a rolling cloud of dust
about the same size as six hundred and fifty-two
thousand banana cream pies.

"Uh-oh. Let's make sure we don't do anything to get him too mad," Sir Ollie double-gulped.

"You got that right, Sir Knight," Sir Seth instantly agreed.

Ooz simply sneered a slightly slimier smile and slid down the dino's long Snactisaurus rex neck. "Now! I have some very, very special news for you and you and you and you…and yes, you, the dog over there!" He paused grandly to let the suspense build up. "You're lookin' at the soon-to-be King Ooz, ruler of the about-to-be Kingdom of Ooztralia!'

Everyone was so shocked right down to the soles of their socks, they all forgot to faint. Or react in any way at all.

"Uh…did you just say King Ooz?" Sir Ollie gasped in complete disbelief.

"You're t'king of t'kingdom o' whut?" Pho Phum gasped even louder.

"Ooztralia?" Sir Seth gasped even louder than that. "Where's that?"

"Look around you, my tattery, tinfoil friend!" Ooz roared with delight. "By this time tomorrow, Claire will no longer exist! And in its place will be the great new Kingdom of Ooztralia!"

Sir Ollie leaned over to Sir Seth. "Uh…the whole thing? Gone?"

"Well, that's what he thinks," Sir Seth whispered, "but he doesn't realize he's up against…"

Sir Ollie closed his fist firmly around El Gonzo
and began to finish Sir Seth's sentence for him.
"The Mighty Knights of—"

"No, no! Not yet," Sir Seth cautioned quietly. "First,
let's find out what his plans are. Then we'll move in."

Sir Ollie knew he was right. "Yeah. Good thinkin',
Sir Seth. And I bet he knows where the princess is, too."

"Claire will never be yers!" Pho roared with disgust.
"Jes take a look and see whut yuh done t' this desert!"

Ooz walked over and stood menacingly in front of Pho.
"You heard me right, my fuzzy-faced friend. I said 'the
Kingdom of Ooztralia.' And by this time tomorrow, I'll be
the king—just as soon as I can return to Castle Claire for
the crowning."

He threw an ax into the sand, barely missing Pho Phum's
foot.

"And there's nothin' you can do to stop me!"

With that, Ooz whirled and walked up to Sir Seth and
Sir Ollie. "And you...you laughable, little taped-up toy
soldiers! You can't stop me either!"

Sir Seth stared the evil little elf straight in the eye.
"You seem to forget, sir," he began softly but firmly, "that
a Mighty Knight is sworn to do whatever he must..."

"To take a wrong and make it a right!" Sir Ollie finished
just as softly, and just as firmly. "And what have you done
with Princess Sundra Neeth?"

Ooz had saved his snidest, evilest sneer for just this
occasion. "Ah yes, the pretty little princess. Well, have

no fear, my tiny, tinny friend. Soon she shall safely be in my hands. In fact, Grak and I were just on our way to, ahem, 'save' her," he said, snickering. "So I insist, please join us. It's so much safer riding up there on Grak than walking down here on foot."

Sir Seth looked at Sir Ollie. And Sir Ollie looked at Sir Seth. No doubt they were sharing the same uncomfortable thought—somehow, they had to stop Ooz. But how do you stop a dino the size of two billion banana cream pies with nothing but a beat-up old broomstick?

There was only one thing to do: until they could come up with a Mighty Knightly Escape Plan, they'd just have to go along with the ogrely Ooz.

But first, they had to come up with Mighty Knightly Plan Number Two—they had to find some way to warn the princess.

Lost and Alone

Princess Sundra Neeth's throat was so desperately dry she could scarcely speak. Or squeak. Or cry. And unfortunately for her, there was hardly anyone in the Sadlands that could have heard her if she could speak or squeak or cry. Except for Ooz and Grak. Or those mysterious Mighty Knights. And so far, she hadn't been able to find any of them.

Wearily, she slumped down on a sun-bleached boulder and looked hopelessly, copelessly down and around in every direction.

"Now what will you do?" Princess Sundra sighed sadly to herself. "Here you are, alone in the middle of a desert, with no idea where you are..."

Just then, the boulder beneath her shifted slightly.

"Hey," a voice said, "get offa my head, willyuh?"

The princess quickly cleared her throat and turned completely around

on the rock. "Did somebody just say something?"

"I certainly did!" the rock said, in a bit of a snit.
"I said: 'Get offa my head.'"

"I didn't know rocks could talk," Sundra started to say,
but the rock interrupted her.

"Obviously, you've never been outside the castle.
Out here in the Sadlands, all the rocks can talk. There's
nothing else out here to do but gossip all day! Haven't
you heard about the Hot Rock Hotline?" the rock said
rather rudely. "That's how we keep busy—spreading
the latest juicy news all over the desert."

"The Hot Rock Hotline? I've never heard of that
either."

"Hmmmmm, it seems to me there's a lot of things
you don't know about a lot of things," the rock chided
her snidely. "So tell me, what are you doing out here
all alone in the desert, dressed in that silly yellow frock,
looking as though you're off to a tea party with the
queen?"

"I'm looking for that evil, awful little elf they call Ooz,"
she said, beginning to get indignantly angry now.

The rock snuffled at the thought. "You want to see
Ooz? Whatever for?"

"To make him unblock the River Claire!"

The snuffle became a guffaw. "Do you really think you
can do that?"

"Yes!" she said with firm determination.

The rock continued to snuffle. "Don't be so silly. Go

back to the castle, where you belong. Ooz will chop you up and feed you to Grak for dessert."

Princess Sundra began to wonder—all over again—what she had gotten herself into. Her problems seemed to be getting bigger instead of better. Still, she stiffened with purpose and proudly proclaimed, "If everyone keeps telling me what I can and can't do, I'll never learn how to do anything for myself. Now, where I can find Ooz?"

"You still want to go!" the rock gasped, completely aghast. "Well, he lives waaaay over there, in a dank, dark cave beyond those distant dunes…but no one dares to go there. Not even me."

"Yes," the princess snickered, "that would be quite a feat for someone without any feet. But as you can see, I do have feet. So if you'll excuse me…"

"Not that he's the most trustworthy sort, but I'd wait for Pho Phum the Fibb, if I were you," the rock interrupted. "You need a guide, and nobody knows the desert better than him."

"Pho Phum?" the princess wondered out loud. "Who's he? What's a Fibb?"

"He's that little black dot out there," said the rock, "and that's his son, Phee, flying on a condor, dumping that bucket of sand on a sandragon. They're both Fibbs. They know these sands like the backs of their hands."

The princess squinted into the shifting, drifting yellow sea of sand. And yes, yes, yes! There was definitely something moving out there. Way, way, way, far, far away on the other side of the desert, there were five small specks—the same color as the big black polka dots on her satiny yellow dress.

The princess turned back to the rock. "Who else's out there with the Fibbs?"

"Well now, let me see," the rock said, trying to lean farther forward. "It looks like them three Otherlanders to me. They're the hot topic on the Hot Rock Hotline right now."

Princess Sundra Neeth brightened slightly. "Oh, you mean Sir Seth, Sir Ollie, and Shasta?"

"Yup. Them. And they seem to be wandering this way…"

"Oh goody! They'll be able to help me stop Ooz." She paused for moment. "For such a grumpy old clump of granite, you've actually been most helpful. Thank you." She flopped down in the shade beside the rock. "Now, if you don't mind, I think I'll wait here for Pho Phum and the Mighty Knights."

"Be my guest. Anything's better than going out there alone in the desert."

The princess laid back and rested her sunbaked, sand-caked eyes…and sighed a huge inside sigh of relief. At last, it seemed everything was beginning to get a little bit better. Sir Seth and Sir Ollie would help her devise a Mighty Knightly plan to unblock the river and once and for all oust Ooz from the land. But just as

Princess Sundra was beginning to smile for the first time since dropping the water bomb on Sir Seth's head, a sudden shout tore her away from her thoughts.

"OH NO!" cried the rock. "LOOK!"

"What...what's wrong?" she wondered, with a sudden wobbly, worried warble in her voice.

"That's what's wrong," the rock gasped aghast all over again. "IT'S GRAK!"

Perching herself once again atop the talking rock, Princess Sundra Neeth stood up and shielded her eyes from the slowly settling sun way over in the west to get a better look. Her heart jumped all the way up to her throat. Out there in the endless shimmering, glimmering sea of sand, she spotted a large globular blob slowly looming larger and larger as it drew nearer and nearer. It was the biggest, blobbiest, most mountainous monster she'd ever seen.

"Oh my," she gasped. "That...is Grak? He's bigger—by far—than Sir Duncan said he would be." She thought about it for a moment, then gasped all over again. "In fact, he's even bigger than that!"

With growing wariness, the princess squinted into the busily shimmering haze. And seated way, way, waaaaay high up on top of the lumbering Snactisaurus rex, the little speck definitely looked like Ooz—of that, there was absolutely no doubt. Because no one else, anywhere, looked anything like Ooz.

The princess squinted even harder, trying to make out

the other faces. Ah yes, seated behind Ooz were those two Otherland knights, Sir Seth and Sir Ollie, plus their dog, Shasta, which Sir Seth called his horse. Behind them, were two strange-looking, bearded little men who looked as though their matted mops had just exploded but somehow managed to stay on their heads.

"How completely…convenient," the princess said to herself, not really believing it. "Think, think, think, Princess! You need a plan. What to do? What to do?"

And that's when, from his perch high atop Grak, Ooz saw the princess and waved to her.

"Ahhhhh, Your Highness," his gruff, gritty growl drifted across the desert. "We've been looking everywhere for you. It's a good thing we found you before it got dark."

Princess Sundra instantly remembered his evil, awful voice from Castle Claire and shuddered at the thought. But then, with a surge of sudden resolve, she drew herself up and decided right then and right there that the fair Queendom of Claire would never, ever in a million years belong to Ooz—no matter what!

"Found me?" she snorted indignantly. "What makes you think that I think that I'm lost? I'm here to tell you that Claire isn't for you to just take!"

Ooz held up one hand. "Oh, but of course not. You misunderstand me. Just stay where you are," he rasped. "We'll come there and have a nice chat about—"

But in the middle of this sentence, a desperate knight-like voice quickly contradicted what the little man had just said. "No, no! Your Highness, don't trust him! RUN! Get back to the castle! Ooz just wants—"

That's as far as Sir Seth got before his frantic plea was abruptly cut off.

Everything was happening so quickly, the princess didn't have time to think. She knew she shouldn't stay where she was, but because she didn't know where she was, she didn't know what else to do.

"Please, Mister Rock, what should I do?"

The rock cleared its throat with a dry ahem. "Well, it's really none of my business," it began. "So let me simply say...whatever you do and wherever you go, don't ever trust Ooz. And never trust a Fibb either."

"Thank you. I shall remember that..."

Princess Sundra looked back once more at the approaching caravan and instinctively began to run as fast as her feet could fly. Suddenly a furious flurry of whapping and flapping wings threw up a choking cloud of sand all around her! She whirled and looked straight into the eyes of an enormous ugly condor. Riding on top was a young girl about the same age as herself.

The princess rubbed the dirt from her eyes. "Who... are you?!"

The young girl smiled a friendly smile and held out her hand. "Hi. I be Pho Phum's daughter, Phi. Come on, we gotta hurry. Come wit' me."

Remembering the rock's recent warning about not trusting the Fibbs, the princess eyed Phi suspiciously. "Thank you, but...um, where are we going?"

Phi avoided her question. "Hurry, git on. Have y'ever rode a condor b'fore?"

That's when Sundra noticed that there were, in fact, two of the big birds, standing, waiting, side by side. "No, I haven't. But before we go anywhere, you still haven't told me...where we are going."

Phi Phum fidgeted with the big bird's reins, still avoiding Sundra's question. "I'll tell you on t'way. We don't got time t'talk 'bout it 'ere."

The princess looked searchingly into Phi's squinty little eyes. "You'll have to show me how to fly."

Phi held up one of the stirrups. "It's easy. Y'jes put yer foot in 'ere," she smiled. "Then y'hang on t'the tether and y'steer 'er jes like she's a horse, don'tcha know."

The princess put her foot in the stirrup and paused, as two thousand new thoughts ran through her mind at exactly the same time.

So she quickly made a quick "Tick List" of her choices:

1. She could go with Ooz...but the rock had told her not to trust Ooz. And Sir Seth had warned her not to trust Ooz. That meant going with Ooz was a NO.

2. She could run off by herself, but she didn't want to be all alone in the middle of the desert in the middle of the night. So running away was also a NO.

3. Or she could fly off with Phi. Who was a Fibb...

Without another word, Princess Sundra took a deep breath and slipped her left foot into the stirrup and swung herself lithely and lightly up onto the back of the big bird as though she had done it ten thousand times before. Then she looked over at Phi.

"I'm ready. Let's go wherever we're going."

Once again, Phi avoided what she said. "This be Babs," she explained quickly. "She be my father's bird, don'tcha know. So when y'talk t'er, call 'er by name. She'll like yuh fer that..."

But before Phi Phum could finish, the princess's condor spread its huge wings and took off.

From high, high up in the sky, Princess Sundra could see it—the magnificent Castle Claire. Her home. For the brightest, briefest bit of a moment, she wondered if Phi was taking her home...but then, almost as soon as the castle had come into view, the two big birds began heading away from it. Heading north—deeper into the dreaded deserted desert of the Sadlands.

"But we're going the wrong way," the princess cried.

Phi Phum didn't even turn her head. "How can we be goin' t'wrong way when yuh don't know where we're goin'?"

Immediately, Princess Sundra Neeth had a terrible sinking feeling—the rock had been right. She had made the mistake of trusting a Fibb.

10 The Great Escape

As the sun was hovering on the horizon, the lurching caravan finally arrived at Ooz's creepy, crawly cave somewhere out there in the middle of the swirling, sunny Sadlands.

Ooz slid down Grak's long Snactisaurus rex neck and stood waiting for the Mighty Knights and their two scruffy Fibb friends to slide down beside him. Then he pointed at the open mouth of his cave.

"In y'go," was all he said as he took their swords and lances and threw them into the roaring inferno that Grak was eagerly rekindling under his gigantic cauldron.

"Oh no!" Sir Ollie gasped. "El Gonzo is...gone!"

"HAH! You won't need no swords when you're Chopped Knight Delight." The evil little elf grinned as he pushed the two windblown warriors into the dark open mouth of the cave.

Suddenly, the only light anywhere in sight was the eerie yellow light from the fire outside, dancing weirdly and wildly on the far wall. Other than that, the cave was as dark as the inside of Sir Seth's closet when he was playing Betcha-Can't-Find-Me with Shasta. And the whole place smelled sorta like wet wooly socks.

Without any warning, Ooz's sandpapery hands roughly grabbed Sir Seth and whirled him around until he was standing beside Sir Ollie. The little man quickly

tied the two knights' wrists together with a thick piece of rope that also smelled like a lot like wet wooly socks. Then he did the same with Pho and Phee Phum, tying them all in one endless face-to-face, wrist-to-wrist circle that seemed impossible to wriggle free from.

"So! You call yourselves Mighty Knights, do yuh? HAH!" he sneered, silhouetted by the dancing flames outside the door. "Well, you don't look so mighty or knightly—or frightening—to me! But you do look a little bit lonely. So stay where you are. I'll go get someone to keep you company..." And with that, the little man whirled and stomped out of sight.

The minute Ooz was gone, Sir Seth quickly said, "Okay, everybody kneel down."

"Huh?" Sir Ollie wondered out loud. "What's up?"

"Just kneel down. You, too, Mister Phum. And Phee, you, too, please."

Without another word, they all knelt down as best

they could. Then Sir Seth said what he always said when he gave Shasta her dinner: "C'mon, girl! Get over here and chew 'em up!" He urged his faithful steed, holding out his wrists to her as best he could. "Hurry up. C'mon, chew 'em up. Chew 'em up."

In her clever canine way, Shasta instantly understood what Sir Seth wanted. "Chew 'em up" meant undo the rope! She began chewing and tugging at the knot on the rope around Sir Seth's wrists.

"Good girl, Shasta! Keep chewing," Sir Seth encouraged her. "We've got to get out of here—like, right now or even sooner than that!"

"At least Ooz didn't catch the princess," said Sir Ollie.

"That's right!" Pho Phum shouted proudly from beside him while Phee grinned in agreement. "I told ya me daughter, Phi, was lookin' out fer us in the sky. Rescued t'princess she did!"

"But don't forget," said Sir Seth, "we've still got to escape!"

Pho Phum simply grunted as he thought about the problem. "B'fore we can do anything, we gotta get 'round that dino out there—he be ten times t'size of a mountain!"

Just then, Shasta gave the rope one last mighty tug— and the knot moved, then moved a little bit more, until it finally came undone!

Sir Seth worked his hands free and scratched Shasta behind both ears at once. "Good girl! There'll be bickies at bedtime for you tonight." Even horses will sometimes have a bickie, if they're hungry enough.

"Now, where wuz we?" Pho Phum grunted as he pulled the rest of ropes from his hands and scratched his head. "Oh yeah...someone has t'keep Grak busy while t'rest of us sneaks off into t'desert."

"Okay," Sir Seth agreed. "So who's gonna do what?"

"Well," the little Fibb said slowly, "seems t'me, it be bes' if Phee and me stays 'ere t'distract Grak while you and Sir Ollie..."

But before Pho Phum could say anything more, they heard Ooz's voice coming down into the cave. He was back already! Everyone immediately put their hands back by their sides as though they were still tied. And smiled great big innocent smiles. Just in case the evil little elf could see them in the deep dark of the cave.

But when Ooz came around the corner, their smiles all changed to a deep group gasp. Because in front of Ooz was his new prisoner—Princess Sundra Neeth!

"Oh no! It's the princess!" Sir Ollie whispered to Sir Seth. "How did Ooz..."

"I don't know," Sir Seth said. "But this looks bad."

Pho stood in silent shock. He couldn't understand how Ooz had captured the princess after he saw her escape with his daughter, Phi.

"So my poor lost princess," Ooz continued, "I'm leaving for Castle Claire to have the Queendom of Claire signed over to...ME! You stay here with your silly little tin-foilly friends and the Fibbs till I get back."

Having said that, he tied the princess to a metal ring on the wall of the cave and stood menacingly over everyone with his ax in his hand. "And don't even think of tryin' to escape across the desert at night—'cause if a sandragon don't get you, for sure Grak will. He can run faster than all of you put together. Times ten."

And with that, he lopped off a lock of Princess Sundra Neeth's hair with his ax, then whirled and stomped out of the cave.

When Ooz was too far away to hear, Sir Seth leaned over and whispered into Princess Sundra's ear: "Your Highness, I'm Sir Seth Thistlethwaite and this is—"

"Oh, I know who you are," the princess interrupted, with a mischievous smile. "I remember the top of your head very well. But as for these two"— Sundra's eyes darkened as she eyed the Fibbs—"never trust a Fibb!!"

"P-p-princess!" stammered Pho Phum. "Whut're yuh sayin'?"

"That I was brought here by a scheming Fibb!" the princess quickly cut him off. "Her name was Phi!"

"My Phi?" Pho said, looking away from the princess.

"Princess!" said Sir Ollie, jumping in. "Pho and Phee sure are kind of weird, but they've been helping us."

"And you're sure of that, Sir Knight?" Sundra said, drawing closer to Sir Ollie. "Sure you can trust them?"

Sir Seth spoke quietly. "Your Highness, I don't know why Phi would do such a thing, but we can't let Ooz ransom you for the entire Queendom of Claire! We've got to get out of here and back to the castle! And to do that, we need all the help we can get."

Sundra sighed and thought. And thought some more. "Well," she said finally, "I do trust *you*, Mighty Knights of Right & Honor. So what do we do?"

"Well, Sir Ollie and I are working on a Mighty Knights plan..." Sir Seth started to say as Shasta began loosening the rope on the princess's wrists.

"To escape!" the princess excitedly finished his sentence, already utterly thrilled at the thought of being part of their knightly adventures. "So tell me quick... what's your plan?"

Sir Ollie became suddenly shy and tongue-tied in front of the princess. "Uh, well, we thought maybe someone could d-d-do something to, uh, sorta get Grak's attention?"

The princess's eyes lit up with deliciously devilish glee. "Oh, that sounds like good fun to me! Besides, I have a few things I'd like to discuss with Mister Grak myself."

And just like that—before Sir Ollie could explain her actual part in the plan—the princess was off.

"Oh no!" Pho Phum said, nervously looking around the dark cave. "Where'd she go?"

"Yeah, wasn't she s'posed t'stay 'ere wit' us?" Phee wondered.

"Come on, everybody, let's get out there!" Sir Seth suggested, and he headed for the mouth of the cave.

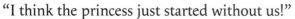

"I think the princess just started without us!"

Outside, Princess Sundra Neeth had already made her way out to the bubbling, voluminous vat where Grak was busily preparing his stew. She looked all the long way up—suddenly seriously awed by his considerable size—then nervously cleared her throat. "Um, excuse me, Mister Grak. I was wondering if I might, um, have a word with you..."

Amid the shuffling thunder of his size 1,404 feet, the mountainous Snactisaurus rex turned and looked down at the princess as the Mighty Knights and the Fibbs watched in open-mouthed awe.

"Uh...who are you?" he wondered in his earthquake baritone voice (for even though Ooz had told him about the prisoners, he rarely paid attention to anything while he was stirring his cauldron).

"I'm-I'm-I AM Princess Sundra Neeth!" she said

more surely now, upset that she had showed any nervousness at all.

Grak leaned even closer. "You're a princess?"

"Yes, I am and..." She tried to find the right words as she slowly began edging her way to the right, which gave the Mighty Knights their chance to escape into the desert—because as she turned, Grak automatically turned with her. Until his back was facing the cave.

At once, Sir Seth realized what the princess was doing. He urgently motioned to Sir Ollie. "C'mon, let's get going while the going's good."

"And leave Princess Sundra here—with Grak? I don't think so."

"You don't understand," Sir Seth whispered frantically. "The princess is distracting Grak on purpose. She's giving us the chance to get away. So c'mon...let's go."

Sir Ollie stiffened with Mighty Knightly pride. "No! A Mighty Knight doesn't run off and leave a princess behind, no matter what..."

Pho put his hand on Sir Ollie's sleeve. "Off y'go, son. Y'gotta stop Ooz. Phee and me'll stay here and look after t'princess."

"But...!"

"Sir Ollie—I dunno why Phi did whut she did, but y'can trust these Fibbs. Now, git goin'. Both o'yuh!"

And so Sir Seth, Sir Ollie, and Shasta crept off in the shadows, leaving the giant Grak leaning even closer down toward Sundra, until his nose was almost touching hers.

"So what's a princess doin' out here in the desert?" he huffed. "All alone? And at night?"

"I, um, I wanted to talk to you about..." the princess began. "Well, I'd like to know why you want to turn my beautiful country into a desert!"

Princess Sundra closed her eyes tightly, sure her outburst was about to get her eaten alive.

But instead, Grak sat back. "Huh? Whudduyuh mean?"

The princess peeked meekly through her fingers. "Just look around you, Mister Grak. Look what you've done. Thanks to you, there's not one tree in sight."

That did it! Now Grak was upset. "Yeah, well, I gotta eat, too. Just like you! The only difference between you and me is you eat truffles and I eat trees." He growled menacingly as he leaned down, baring his teeth.

The princess put her hands on her hips—if this big dino was going to make her his latest snack, she'd at least speak her mind! "Well, keep that up and soon there won't be ANYTHING left in this country except dead, dried-up desert! And when that happens, then what will you eat, you big DUMMY?!"

As soon as Sundra finished speaking, her hands flew over her mouth. There was no way Grak would put up with that—she was dino dinner, for sure. Sundra closed her eyes and waited. And waited. And waited some more. Then, so scared she nearly shook the polka dots off her dress, she gently opened one eye.

But the big hulk was just standing there, thinking. Thinking very slowly.

"Oh," he said eventually. "I never thought about that..."

Meanwhile, like birds in the night, the Mighty Knights and their smiling, wagging horse took this opportunity to scurry down the hill and out into the silently waiting desert. Then they paused and waited while their eyes got used to the bright silver moonlight on the sand.

"What are you doing out here? At night?" A small voice startled them.

They all looked down into a pair of knee-high blue eyes, while Shasta cautiously nosed closer for an introductory sniff.

"Who are you?" Sir Ollie asked.

"I'm Glug. A chuggamugga bug, just out gatherin' some cool evening dew. So that's who I am. Now, who are you?"

Both Sir Seth and Sir Ollie broke into big, relieved

grins. Glug was one of the water-gathering bugs that Pho Phum had told them about. In the bright moonlight, Glug's sand-colored skin was such an exact match for the sand-colored sand he was standing on that all Sir Seth could really see were two big blue eyes. But even in daylight, few can tell where a chuggamugga bug ends and the desert begins. So suffice it to say, it looks a lot like a sand-colored ant, except quite a bit larger, with big blue eyes and two tall antennas on top of its head that aren't antennas at all, but two long, bendy drinking straws.

"Uh...are you the Otherlanders we've been hearing about?"

"Yes," Sir Ollie smiled. "And we need your help."

Suddenly, another pair of knee-high blue eyes appeared. "You need help?" a second chuggamugga asked. "Can we help you?"

"Yes, you can," Sir Seth said, relieved. "But first...we need a drink!"

As the Mighty Knights greedily slurped up their first drink since leaving the castle, they skimmed through the sad saga of how Ooz was trying to take over the Queendom of Claire. And as they spoke, more knee-high blue eyes arrived. Then a few more. And two score after that. Until a sea of knee-high blue eyes were listening intently to their every word.

"Ooz wants to take over Claire?" Glug exclaimed at the end of the story. "He wouldn't dare!"

"Oh yes, he does dare!" Sir Ollie said firmly.

"How can we help?" everyone immediately shouted.

Sir Seth looked the chuggamuggas right in the eye. "It's simple: we've got to get to the castle before Ooz does."

"Across the desert?" one of the bugs gasped.

"On foot?" another gasped even louder than that.

The sea of knee-high blue eyes just stared at one another.

"I don't know," one of the chuggamugga bugs finally said. "No one here has ever crossed the whole desert in one night before."

That pretty well ended the conversation. There was a long pause while everyone thought of what to say next.

"What about those funny-looking birds you were riding today?" Princess Sundra Neeth asked from somewhere behind them.

"Princess Sundra Neeth!?" a chorus of chuggamuggas cried out at once. "What are you doing in the desert?"

"At night?"

"On foot?"

"Your Highness! How did you get away from Grak?" Sir Ollie asked with surprise.

Princess Sundra smiled. "Maybe I can trust some Fibbs after all! Pho and Phee took over distracting Grak. When I slipped away, Pho was trying to get him to try a new diet or something." She giggled and looked at Sir Seth and Sir Ollie. "You know, that dino maybe super-double scary, but he's not all that smart."

The princess suddenly looked all around her at the sea of knee-high blue eyes. "But, um, just before we find our

way back to the castle, there's something I should do..."
She walked over to Glug, then knelt down on one knee
and put out her hand. "I've never met a chuggamugga
before, Mister Bug. How do you do?"

"How-how-how do I do what, Your Highness?" replied
Glug, the knocking of his knees almost drowning out his
wobbling, never-met-a-for-real-princess-before voice.

The princess smiled and leaned closer. "How do you
survive out in these dry, dreary Sadlands, day after day?"

By now, poor old Glug was so completely agog, he
almost passed out. "Well, Your Highness, I sur-sur-survive
out here, day after day, by going out only at n-n-night."

"Of course. Thank you, Mister Bug," Princess Sundra
said kindly, getting back up. "I never knew there were
talking rocks and chuggamugga bugs and so many others
out here. One day, not far away, I'll be the new queen
of Claire—and when I am, I'm going make sure these
Sadlands become glad again. The kind of beautifully
grand and green place that you chuggamuggas can
happily go out in, day or night. Does that sound right?"

"Oh y-y-yes, Your Highness," said Glug with a grin.

"Sorry to interrupt, Princess," Sir Ollie began, "but I
think you had a good idea back there about those funny-
looking birds—the umbies! Hey, Sir Seth, didn't Pho say
something about the umbies hiding at some grotto?"

"Umm...not Gorgon Grotto?" Glug said warily. "I
wouldn't go there if I were you."

"Yeah, Gorgon Grotto!" Sir Ollie echoed. "Why not?"

Glug shrugged. "It's a grotto where the Gorgons live."

"So? What's a Gorgon?"

"If I tell you, you won't want to go."

"Of course I'll go," Sir Ollie said, slightly unsure.

"Well, a Gorgon's pretty unpretty, y'know."

"Yeah. So?"

Glug couldn't stop himself from smiling. "I mean, a Gorgon's very, very scary..."

"Yeah. And?"

"Well, Gorgons have snakes all over their heads instead of hair!"

Sir Ollie's suntan instantly turned white. "Snakes!" he gasped, then he scrambled to recover. "Yeah, well, I've seen lotsa Gorgons before, y'know. They don't scare me much."

"Really?!" Glug leaned forward. "Because some people say a Gorgon's so scary that just one look can turn you to...stone."

"Stone?" Sir Ollie gasped all over again. "Y'mean, I'll turn into a...statue of me?"

Sir Seth stood up. "Come on, everyone. Princess. Shasta. It's time to get going." He turned to Glug. "How far is it to Gorgon Grotto? Will you show us the way?"

"You did hear that part about the 'turning to stone'?" Glug confirmed.

Sir Seth nodded.

"Okay," Glug shrugged. "I don't know what you're gonna do when you get there, but follow me."

11 Gorgon Grotto

Sir Seth stopped in front of the gaping black mouth of eerie Gorgon Grotto and looked down at Glug. Then he looked back into the black cave. Inside, the grotto was as dark as a dog's nose, without even the teeniest, tiniest trickle of light anywhere in sight.

"Well, this is Gorgon Grotto." Glug shuddered, peeking inside. "Some umbies are sleeping in there somewhere."

"Yeah? How do you know?" Sir Ollie wondered from behind him.

"Oh, don't worry. They're in there, all right," Glug began to explain. "Y'see, the umbies and the Gorgons have this great Get-Along Agreement, which means they all get along great. During the day, the umbies make cream of cactus soup and rattlesnake sandwiches for the Gorgons to eat. To return the favor, the Gorgons guard all the umbies while they're sleeping at night. And nobody gets turned into stone. So everyone's happy, all day and all night. But don't get too excited—the Gorgons aren't nearly that nice to anyone else."

Princess Sundra came up beside them. "I hope they don't mind visitors arriving this late."

Glug shrugged again. "You'll just have to go in there and find out."

"Go in there?" Sir Seth repeated nervously, leaning in for a closer look.

"Yep. If you want to talk to an umbie, that's where they are."

"Be careful," Sir Ollie cautioned him. "If you see a Gorgon, try not to look at it. You don't want to be turned into a statue."

Sir Seth gulped a mighty gulp and put one foot inside the grotto. Then stopped. "Um...yoo-hoo? Anyone home?"

Not a sound emerged from the inky, deathly still darkness.

Beside him, Shasta leaned in as far as she could possibly lean without falling flat on her nose. And behind her, Sir Ollie was doing the same.

"Uh, sorry to bother you, but...are there any umbies in here?"

Still not a sound came from inside the grim, ghastly grotto.

Sir Seth took one more step and paused again, letting his eyes get used to the dark. Then, from out of nowhere and with no kind of warning whatever—and without making any other sound—a mega-quadruple, heavy-duty, hideous snake-headed face shot out of the darkness, stopped about four inches in front of a startled Sir Seth, and shrieked at the top of its hideous voice:

"WHAT DO YOU WANT?"

And from that day to this, the rumor abounds that—for the itty-bittiest fraction of a second—Sir Seth, Shasta, and Princess Sundra Neeth were just an itty bit nervous as they left the grotto, running as fast as all of their whirling little legs would carry them. And the rumor goes on to say that they would have run even faster that day if they had found eight more legs to run faster with.

Sir Ollie thought for sure he had just been run over by an invisible Snactisaurus rex that he didn't see coming. He sat in the sand, stunned, staring up at the most horrendously horrible grinning face he had ever seen in his entire short life—with two hundred grinning, hissing snakes writhing around all over her head.

"I'm sorry!" the gruesome Gorgon giggled girlishly.

"I must apologize. But there's just so little to laugh about around here, the girls and I couldn't hold ourselves back."

Sir Ollie was so surprised he hadn't been turned into a statue that he just stood there as stiff as a stone, too stunned to speak.

"My name's Saffron." The Gorgon smiled, holding out one hand. "Who are you?"

"Uh, I'm Sir Ollie Everghettz. At your service, ma'am," Sir Ollie finally managed to say as he put out his hand—surprised it still moved.

"Well now, Sir Ollie, why don't you go out there and bring back your friends—if you can find them," Saffron said in an almost normal voice. "I'll go get an umbie and meet you right here." She turned to leave, then turned back. "That's why you came here, isn't it? To talk with an umbie?"

"Yes," Sir Ollie agreed. "But, uh, how come you didn't turn me to stone?"

"Oh, haven't you heard? Gorgons don't do that anymore. It gives us a bad name," Saffron shrieked with laughter. "You're reading too many of those old kids' books." Then she thought about it briefly and added, "But I can, if you want."

"No! No, thank you, ma'am," Sir Ollie smiled. "I like me when I'm all bendy, just the way I am."

"And so do I." Saffron smiled an almost normal smile. "Now, off you go. I'll meet you right here."

"Bye! So long! Seeyuh! Ciao for now, baby! Cheerio! C'mon back soon, y'hear? Nice meeting yuh!" all the snakes said from the top of her head, waving and waggling their separate serpentine goodbyes.

Sir Ollie didn't wait to be coaxed. "Bye!" he said over one shoulder as he dashed off into the moonlit night, in the same direction as the others.

He hadn't gone far when he tripped over Shasta, who had tripped over Glug, who had tripped over Sir Seth when Princess Sundra had fallen down after taking just a few hundred steps.

"Did you hear what she said?" Sir Ollie said excitedly. "She's gonna get the umbies! Come on, we've got to go back to the grotto."

"Go back to the grotto?" Glug gulped. "You've gotta be kidding. You go back to the grotto, then tell me all about it. I'm getting' out of here."

Sir Ollie shrugged. "Hey, Saffron's really nice…for someone with snakes all over her head. And look at me: she doesn't turn people into stone anymore. I think you'll really like her."

The princess got to her feet and dusted off her dress. "If you're afraid to go," she challenged Sir Seth, "I'll go to the grotto by myself. Don't forget, Ooz is already on his way to the castle!"

Red-faced, Sir Seth got to his feet. "We'll all go, Your Highness. But I don't know how anyone could like a face like that."

The four of them made their way back up to the gaping black mouth of the grotto, where Saffron was sitting, waiting for them. The full moon was now moving high in the eastern sky, adding more silvery light to brighten their way.

"The umbies are in there, but they don't want to be bothered," Saffron said with a sigh. "Why don't you go in and give it a try?"

They all paused at the mouth of the cave and cautiously looked in. Inside, the grotto was still as black as ever, but from somewhere deep, deep inside, the hollow sound of echoing voices could barely be heard. The Mighty Knights braced themselves in case another one of those ghoulish Gorgons jumped at them again, shrieking like a banshee. But instead, a sleepy-eyed umbie poked its head out.

"Um, do you want to see me?" it said with a yawn.

"Yes!" the princess answered for everyone. "I realize it's terribly late, but we need you and your friends to take us to Castle Claire—tonight! Before Ooz can get there and take over the entire Queendom of Claire for himself."

"You want to go to Castle Claire...tonight?" the umbie interrupted, looking off to the south.

Two other umbies arrived and gasped at the thought.

"Across the desert?"

"At night?"

"On foot?" Yet another jumped in.

"Yes. No matter what, we must get there tonight!" Princess Sundra begged them. "Will you take us?"

"I'm afraid not," the first umbie flatly refused. "As you can plainly see, we're rather busy right now."

"Busy?" Sir Seth laughed. "Doing what?"

"Trying to sleep!"

And with that, the umbie disappeared into the back of the cave—and would have slammed the door behind her, if there had been a door there to shut.

Indignantly, and in a bit of a royal snit, Princess Sundra put her hands on her hips. "So! That's the way you want it, is it?" she huffed. "Well, sometimes, one must do what one must..."

She walked boldly up to the gaping mouth of Gorgon Grotto, took a deep breath, then bellowed at the top of her lungs in a most un-princess-like voice:

"HEY! WAKE UP!!"

Her voice echoed and re-echoed—then echoed some more—rebounding off the hard stone walls of the cave for a full four minutes or more, before a stumbling, grumbling, sleepy-eyed umbie reappeared at the door. Then two more. Then four. Then more and more and more. Even three grumpy Gorgons showed up as well.

"What do you mean 'Wake up'?'" the umbie groaned. "Can't you see it's nighttime out there?"

The princess leaned forward until her nose was almost touching the end of the umbie's. "Well, it's time three of you got up to help us save the Queendom of Claire. Or I'll stand here shouting 'Wake up' all night!"

"Very well, you win," the umbie grumbled. "I'll see if I can find three volunteers..."

"Well, hurry along. We're wasting time!" the princess said edgily. "We've got to get going."

The umbie looked down its long, hang-down nose at her. "Yes, yes, I'm sure you must. But first, we must discuss payment."

"Right!" another agreed.

"To cross the desert, don't forget."

"At night."

"And on foot."

By now, Princess Sundra was so frustrated, she began bellowing all over again. "I'll pay you double your usual fee. But we must leave here immediately!"

"Double the fee?" Saffron suddenly perked up. "For two rattlesnake sandwiches, I'd take you there myself, but I'm afraid my hair is an absolute fright!"

Finally, the three sleepy-eyed umbies formed up in front of the grotto, yawning and grumbling and mumbling and complaining, but ready to go. Then the gallant crusaders—Sir Seth with Shasta, Sir Ollie, and the Princess—clambered aboard, and the odd-looking caravan walked slowly out into the endless silvery desert.

"We're off," Sir Ollie said excitedly, looking over at Sir Seth.

"Well, for sure it's a start," Sir Seth agreed slowly. "But we've got a lot of pretty quick catching-up to do if we're ever going to beat Ooz to the castle."

Sir Ollie just nodded, now a little too worried to say anything. There had to be a faster way to get to the castle. But how?

12 A Flight to Catch

With an ax clenched firmly in each hand, Ooz the evil, awful elf trudged wearily, one foot in front of the other, across the cold, deserted silvery sand. He finally slumped down on a rock, emptied the sand from his shoes, and looked all around.

"The desert's so beautiful at night, isn't it?" a voice said from nearby.

"You call this beautiful?" Ooz grumbled without bothering to look. He knew the voice belonged to one of the endlessly babbling rocks that were dotted out there all over the desert.

The voice paused, trying to think of something else to say. "Ahhhhh, yes, yes, yes. And believe it or not, I can remember the times when everything was even more beautiful than this..."

Ooz didn't bother to answer, because he knew what was coming next.

"With trees and green grass and flowers everywhere, and a long, lazy river winding its way down the middle."

"Ohhhhh, will you stop it! Stop it! Stop it! I'm so weary of hearing the same old thing over and over again, it makes me want to chop off the end of your tongue." Ooz angrily jumped to his feet and, with one deft, lightning-like swing, chopped the babbling rock cleanly in half.

Which now meant there were two talking rocks, instead of just one.

"So as we were saying, the Sadlands used to be green fields and fine forests," both rocks continued to say at the same time.

"I told you to STOP it!" Ooz shouted, swinging both axes at once.

Which meant now there were four talking rocks, instead of just two.

Ooz put on his shoes and headed back out into desert, muttering and grumbling to himself. "Why does everyone always blame me for turning this place into the Sadlands? It's not my fault. Grak ate all the trees, not me! I'm tired of being blamed for what Grak ate, and for—"

Then, suddenly, right in the middle of his sentence, a silent, sinister shadow passed overhead, like a dark cloud, briefly blocking the silvery sky. Ooz quickly looked up to see what it was. Two giant condors were circling slowly overhead, with Phi Phum sitting on one, searching the desert.

"Good!" Ooz growled. "She's come. Just as we planned."

He ran excitedly out into the flats, away from the still-babbling rocks, waving his arms and shouting, "Phi Phum, here I am! Right here!"

The two huge birds immediately dropped from the sky, circling lower and lower until they landed beside the evil little elf. Phi uncrossed her legs and dropped down to the sand.

"Quick! I brought'cha a condor t'ride. Get on. We gotta get goin'," she urged him. "T'princess and her friends is right behind yuh and comin' fast."

Ooz grunted, slid his dusty foot in the stirrup, and pulled himself up onto Phi's father's big bird. "They're coming fast, you say? How could that be? How did they escape my mighty Grak?" he asked, almost overcome by surprise. "And across the desert at night? On foot?"

"They're not comin' on foot," Phi filled him in. "They be ridin' some umbies they got from t'Gorgons."

Ooz sagged and smiled an evil, awful smile. "HAH! They're chasing me on a bunch of stumbling, bumbling, tangle-toed umbies? Good! That means they won't get here till next year. Right now, just show me how I make this thing fly. I must get to the Castle Claire and sign the Magna Charter at once."

"Y'tap 'im wit' yer toes and then off yuh go. Like this." Phi gently nudged the big bird with her bare feet, and at once, her condor responded, spreading its wings and taking to the air. When the other bird saw her take off, it immediately spread its wings and followed.

As the two condors climbed higher and higher into the night sky, Phi looked over at Ooz with a puzzled expression on her face. "Uh, whut's a Magnum Charta?"

"Just a dumb old piece of paper." Ooz dismissed it with a wave of one hand. "It's filled with long, confusing words such as 'henceforth' and 'heretofore,' and other phrases that—once I've signed it—will mean Queen Bea has turned the entire Queendom of Claire over to me. Why do you wanna know?"

Phi thought about it some more, then added, "Oh, I wuz just wonderin', y'know. Do I 'ave t'sign it, too?"

"You? Sign it?" Ooz said again, looking over at her, very suspiciously now.

Phi shrugged. "I dunno how t'read or write."

Ooz immediately smiled another of his evil, oily smiles. "HAH! Don't worry about that! Oh, no, no, no. Just leave all those technical details to me. All you have to do is relax…and next thing you know,

you'll be the proud new part-owner of every grain of sand in the Sadlands! Just as I promised you would."

Phi smiled over at Ooz. "Mister Ooz?"

"Yeah?"

"I jes knew deep down that y'were t'most wunnerful, wunnerful person. I always told me father that if we jes talked to yuh, we could be friends. I jes don't know how t'tank yuh!"

He looked over at Phi with that evil grin. "Ah, but you've already thanked me, my dear. Much more than you know."

"Look! There's t'castle!" Phi cried, pointing down. "We're almost there."

Ooz looked down at the magnificent marble Castle Claire, gleaming silently in the bright moonlight. And he began to drool.

"Ahhhhh, I can almost smell the ink on the Magna Charter already!"

13 There's Just One Problem...

Meanwhile, back in the desert, the Mighty Knights and Princess Sundra Neeth were, unfortunately, finding that riding the umbies was slower than they expected. A lot slower.

"Can't you walk any faster than this?" the princess urged them.

There was a pause while the umbies discussed it a bit. "Fast? What's that?"

They all began milling around, arguing and otherwise wasting precious time.

"Fast? I think it has something to do with speed."

"Fast? Oh no, no. Fasting is something you do instead of eating!"

"Well, personally, I've never tried going anywhere any faster than slow."

Suddenly, Sir Seth had an idea. "Excuse me, but have you ever thought of using your wings? And tried flying?"

The umbie looked at Sir Seth in open-mouthed awe, looking over one shoulder at her lacy, feathery wings. "Flying? So that's what these things are for! I thought wings were things that were there just for shade."

Sir Seth walked up to the umbie and examined one of its large wings. "It's okay, there are some things I don't know either. But one thing I do know for sure: these things are wings. And the reason you've got 'em is so you can fly! Get ready, 'cause we're gonna give 'em a try."

"You'll love it!" the princess eagerly agreed. "Flying is totally, totally amazing!"

Immediately, Sir Ollie and Shasta perked up, remembering an adventure they had once had with their friend Edith-Anne. "Princess Sundra's right! It's, like, excitement times ten!"

The umbie looked down at the two knights and the princess. "How would you know?" it huffed haughtily. "You don't have any wings."

Just as huffily, Sir Ollie stood up on his tippy tiptoes and looked the umbie right in the neck. "Oh yeah? Well, that's because I don't need any wings if my friend already has sloth broth."

"Sloth what?" The umbie cocked its head.

"C'mon, you two, stop wasting time. We've got to get to the castle," Sir Seth reminded them, then he turned back to the umbie. "What's your name, Mister Umbie?"

"My name's Buzz," the umbie announced sheepishly. "My parents said he was the ancient god of flight."

"Buzz? The god of flight? Well, there you go," Sir Seth laughed. "Come on, Sir Ollie, get over here and give me a hand. Let's open Buzz's wings as far as we can—and show me every spare inch of wingspan he's got."

The two Mighty Knights each took a wing and walked it open as far as it would go. When they were done, they stood there, gawking at the awesome expanse of the umbie's huge wings.

Sir Seth swung up onto Buzz's broad back. "Wow. With wings like that, we should get to Castle Claire in one minute flat. Okay, everyone, it's time to stop yappin' and start flappin' instead. Everybody got an umbie? Okay, hop on. Here we go!"

Buzz looked back over one shoulder. "Um, there's just one problem. What do I do now?"

Sir Seth eagerly flapped his arms up and down. "You do this! As fast as you can. And start running at the same time."

"You want me to run?"

"Yeah. Run. It's easy. You just put one foot in front of the other. Then do it faster and faster, and then you start flapping your wings as hard as you can—at the same time."

"At the same time?" Buzz lifted one long, knobbly leg and tried flapping one wing. "Like this?"

With a sinking feeling, Sir Seth realized that not only didn't Buzz know how to fly, but he didn't even know how to run. "Fasten your seatbelts, everybody," he called to his friends. "Something tells me this is going to be a rough flight. C'mon, Shasta," he said, reaching down for his steed. "You'd better ride up here with me."

However, all of the umbies surprised everyone by walking quickly quite well, right from the start—and they managed to keep their huge feet out of one another's way without stumbling or bumbling or tumbling at all.

They were almost ready to hurl themselves magnificently into the air when Sir Ollie's umbie suddenly tripped and dug a long furrow in the sand with the end of its turned-under nose. Which meant everyone had to stop and go back to see if they were all right. Which meant everyone then had to start all over again.

Meanwhile, somewhere out there, Ooz was already in the air and on his way to the castle.

"If we could only get started," a frustrated Sir Ollie said to Sir Seth, "we'd catch up and pass Ooz like he was parked."

Sir Seth sighed and boosted Sir Ollie back onto his still-grumbling umbie. "C'mon. Like I said earlier, we gotta stop yappin' and start flappin'!"

The four umbies lined up in a row and began galloping and flapping all over again. Then, when they were just about ready to soar, one of the umbies once again stumbled and dug another long, frustrating furrow with the end of its turned-under nose. And everyone had to stop and do it all over again.

"Oh no, we'll never get to the castle in time!" the princess sobbed, wringing her hands in despair. "What are we going to do?"

"Well, you could always jump off Jump-Off Rock, up there at the top of Condor Canyon, and glide down from there," a voice said from somewhere nearby. "At least, that's what I'd do if I were you instead of a rock."

"Jump-Off Rock? Why do they call it Jump-Off Rock?" Sir Ollie wanted to know.

"Oh, probably because that's where everyone goes when they want to jump off a rock into Condor Canyon," the rock said very matter-of-factly.

Sir Ollie paled at the thought. "That's a looooong way to jump."

"Maybe so. But it's also the fastest way to get to the castle." The rock would have shrugged if it could. "Besides, Jump-Off Rock is my cousin. I'm Sandy and he's Rocky. Tell Rocky you were talkin' to me. He'll look after you real good. He hangs out over there, looking out over the canyon."

Princess Sundra Neeth immediately perked up. "Oh, Sir Seth, we have no choice. We simply must jump off

Jump-Off Rock. It's the only thing we can do!"

"That's what I was afraid you might say," Sir Seth said nervously, trying not to let it show.

"Um, how far is it to walk to the castle?" Sir Ollie suggested hopefully.

"Too far," the rock said flatly. "You'd never make it in time. Jump-Off Rock's the only way to go."

Sir Seth looked at Sir Ollie. "The princess and the rock are right. Jumping off Jump-Off Rock is the only thing we can do..."

Then Princess Sundra Neeth said it for all of them. "So what are we sitting around talking for? Where's Jump-Off Rock? We've just got to get to the Magna Charter first!"

Sir Seth agreed. "Hang on tight, everybody. Here we go!"

But Sir Ollie was still looking down. "Uh...maybe we should have a vote."

"Okay, let's vote," Sir Seth said with a smile, knowing what the answer would be. "Hands up, everybody who thinks we should jump."

The princess put her hand up. Sir Seth put his hand up. Even Shasta smiled and put up a paw.

"I'll go first," Princess Sundra volunteered.

14 Ooz's Hard Bargain

The two huge condors slipped silently down from the star-sprinkled sky and alit on the lush, cushioned lawn of Castle Claire without making a sound. Ooz looked over at Phi Phum as he slid down from the condor, then he looked up at the hushed, dark castle. Victory was so tantalizingly near, his nubbly little knees were actually knocking. Inside his head, he could hear a clock ticking and talking to him, urgently urging him on: Ooz, you've got to get that charter quick-quick-quick, before the princess and her pots-and-pan pals can get there.

Ooz glanced over at Phi. "Well, well, well"—he sneered his thin evil grin—"everything's so peaceful and quiet around here, I hate to wake everyone up. Stay here and look after the birds. I'll be back before you know that I've gone. In fact, I'll probably be back even sooner than that."

He turned and hurriedly tromped and stomped his way across the long, winding path that ran through the magnificent Royal Claireberry Gardens to the magnificent marbled castle, squishing and squashing and crushing every flower he came to, making more noise than the changing of the guard.

"Halt!" a voice abruptly cut through the hush of the night. "Who are you? And what do you want?"

Ooz whirled and snarled in the general direction of the voice, then continued on in his lead-footed way, flattening all the flowers and each budding shrub he came to without saying a word. But he hadn't taken more than four steps when, all at once, every candle everywhere in the castle was suddenly lit.

Still, Ooz trundled relentlessly through the gorgeous award-winning garden.

"Halt!" a chorus of voices cried out. "Who are you? And what do you want?"

Finally, the evil little elf stopped and roared in his sandpaper voice: "It is me! King Ooz! The new king of the Queendom of Claire. Tell Queen Beatrix to meet me in the Great Hall at once!"

There was a long, stunned silence. Then someone said, "Excuse me, but who did you say you are?"

Ooz roared even louder: "I said I am Ooz! Your new king."

There was another long pause. Then the same voice replied, "Sorry. We don't need one. We already have a queen."

From out of the quickly awakening night, a dozen uniformed guards appeared and formed a circle around Ooz, menacingly barring the way with their long pointed spears. "Come with us!" one of them ordered.

"Come with you? HAH!" the little man roared with growing delight.

"What is going on at this time of night?" a calm voice interrupted.

"Well, well, well, if it isn't wise old Sir Duncan." Ooz sneered and held up an ax. "Tell these toy soldiers who I am before I chop them up and have them for breakfast."

The wise old adviser looked down at Ooz but showed little surprise. "Ah, Mister Ooz. What a pleasure to see you again," Sir Duncan greeted the evil little elf with a warmth he didn't feel. "But is there some reason this meeting can't wait until morning?"

"I said now!" Ooz snarled. "Tell Queen Beatrix to meet us in the Great Hall. We don't have a minute to waste."

"But the queen is—" Sir Duncan began to protest.

"I don't care where the queen is or what she's doing!" Ooz interrupted him. "Tell Her Majesty to come here at once!" Then he paused and sneered. "Tell her I have some good news...about her dear little runaway daughter."

Sir Duncan winced at the thought. "You have news of the princess?"

Ooz was enjoying every glorious moment, and he began dragging out the suspense as long as he dared. He reached into his pocket and held out the lock of hair he had chopped from Princess Sundra's head.

"Do I have 'news' of the princess? HAH!" He sneered his slimey smile. "I have much more than that. I have all of the princess! But don't worry. The princess is safe out there in the Sadlands...with Grak and me."

When he saw the princess's hair, Sir Duncan's hand shot to his mouth in horror. He sighed and reluctantly said, "Guards, allow him to pass. Then alert the queen that Mister Ooz wishes to see her."

Ooz pushed the guards aside and continued tromping and stomping his way through the gorgeous gardens up to the castle. He stormed into the Great Hall and stomped over to the glass cask enshrining the hallowed Magna Charter of the Queendom of Claire and climbed up onto the chair beside it.

"Open it!" he ordered.

Sir Duncan gasped at the thought. "Open the glass cask of the Magna Charter? But—"

"Open it!" Ooz said once again, raising his ax. "Or I'll do it for you."

Sir Duncan wrung his hands in anguish. "But there's only one person in the entire Queendom of Claire who has the key."

"And that person is ME!" Queen Beatrix said from across the Great Hall.

Sir Duncan and Ooz whirled to face the queen, who was, as usual, magnificently dressed. She slowly strode across the floor of the huge, echoing throne room with fiery menace flowing from her angry gray eyes.

"So!" she spoke. "You have news of my daughter, Mister Ooz? Well, be quick about it! In case you hadn't noticed, it's the middle of the night."

With those words, the war and wills between the queen and Ooz had begun.

"Open the cask," he ordered Queen Beatrix with his thin evil grin.

"Do what?" the queen asked, aghast.

"Open the cask"—Ooz continued to smile—"if you ever want to see your daughter again."

The smoldering tension filling the room was suddenly thick enough to cut with a knife. Or an ax.

"What do you mean?" the queen gasped, thrusting her hand to her throat.

"Let's just say, she's living with me and that's the way it's going to be...unless you agree to turn the Queendom of Claire over to me." Ooz sneered from his perch on the chair. "So if you want to see the princess again, all I ask is that you open the cask."

The queen took a deep breath. "And?"

"I simply sign my name at the bottom, which turns the Queendom of Claire and everything in it over to me!

And I will be king of the new Kingdom of Ooztralia!"
He paused to let the threat sink in. "Because only when
I am king will I bring your daughter back to the castle."

For the first time in her life, Queen Beatrix the Sixth
didn't know what to say. So she said nothing. She
reached into the deep pocket of her red-and-gold robe
and closed her hand around the large golden key, then
anxiously turned her sad eyes to Sir Duncan.

"Well, Sir Duncan," she finally said, "what do you
advise?"

It was Sir Duncan's turn to take a deep breath.
"Your Majesty, as I see it, we have no choice," he
solemnly sighed. "We must give him the key and
trust he becomes a better king than the evil elf he is."

Ooz sneered a cynical grin. "Well, well, well,
Sir Duncan, you're smarter than I thought."

With that—and with a tear streaming down both of her cheeks—Queen Beatrix the Sixth knew she had no choice. She couldn't lose her daughter forever.

"You win, you wicked little elf," she said in a voice you could barely hear. She handed Ooz the golden key to the treasured glass cask. He excitedly grabbed the key from her hand, wiggled it nervously in the large golden lock, and desperately threw open the glass door.

And there before him was the magnificent, hallowed Magna Charter of the Queendom of Claire. For a while, he could scarcely speak. The whole room was hushed.

"At last," Ooz finally gasped greedily.

He reached into the open cask…

15 The God of Flight

Sir Seth, Sir Ollie, Princess Sundra, and Shasta all sat on their umbies, teetering unsteadily on the edge of the ledge of Jump-Off Rock. One by one, they nervously looked down at that shocking, knee-knocking drop down into Condor Canyon.

"Actually, it's best if you don't look down," Jump-Off Rock suggested.

"It's even better if I don't come here at all," Sir Ollie suggested, then he looked over at Sir Seth. "Are you cuhhhhh-razy? Do you really think we can jump all that way down there—and live?"

"What're you worried about?" Sir Seth grinned, putting one arm around Sir Ollie's shoulder. "You've already done it once. That's how we got here. Remember falling out of the pipe?"

"I don't want to remember!" Sir Ollie shuddered at the thought. "I had my eyes closed the whole time."

Even Princess Sundra Neeth wasn't her usual feisty self. "Oh dear. Now that I see how far down it is, it is a little bit farther than I thought. Maybe you should go first, Sir Seth."

"Don't worry," Sir Seth told his friends. "We're not going to jump."

Sir Ollie took a deep breath. "We're not?"

"No. We're going to fly there instead," he said, grabbing the reins of his umbie.

"C'mon, Buzz! This is your chance to untangle those things you call wings and start flying."

"Um, well, I..."

Sir Seth pulled himself up onto the umbie's back. "Tallyho! Here we go! What are you—an umbie or a mouse?"

Buzz knew he was trapped. "Um, I'm an umbie!"

"Then be one! Here we go!"

Still too stunned to think or blink, Buzz backed up a couple of steps, then lifted one leg and started running as fast as he could. By the time he got to the lip of the ledge, it was too late to stop. Or to turn. Or to change his mind or do anything else. So he simply closed his eyes.

And JUMPED.

Then Buzz braced himself and waited for the nose-gnashing, bone-bashing crash at the bottom. That didn't come. In fact, being dead, he suddenly said, wasn't nearly as bad as he thought. It was a sort of hushed, serene sensation that certainly didn't hurt very much. In fact, it sort of felt as though he was floating.

Or flying!

Buzz opened his eyes and was completely and utterly too stunned to speak. Then he looked down. And almost fainted right there in midair.

"Buzz! Look at this! You did it! We're flying!" Sir Seth was shouting. "You are the god of flight after all!"

Then they all headed to the castle as fast as the umbies could flap—which might have been fast for an umbie but was not nearly fast enough for the knights and the princess.

Sir Ollie came up beside Sir Seth, grinning from ear to ear. "Who needs sloth broth to be able to fly? We're flyin' just fine up here without it."

Princess Sundra also pulled alongside. "Oh, Sir Seth, the Mighty Knights have surely saved the day. We'll be at the castle in no time now!"

"Well, at least we're finally flying—instead of waddling," Sir Seth said slowly, looking down at the moonlit landscape ahead. "But I still can't see the castle yet. Onward, Mighty Knights!"

Finally, after what seemed like two months and ten days, Sir Ollie whooped a Mighty Knight Secret Two-Caw Alert: "Caw! Caw!"

Immediately, Sir Seth looked where Sir Ollie was pointing. And there was the castle, down there on their right, glistening like a diamond in the night.

"Caw! Caw!" Sir Seth acknowledged, then he looked over at Princess Sundra Neeth. "Okay, Your Highness, get ready—we know that the umbies know how to fly, but now it's time to find out if they know how to dive!" He tapped Buzz on the back of his head. "C'mon, Mister Flyguy, let's see if there's anyone still awake down there in the castle."

Sir Seth looked all around below him, trying to spot Ooz and the condors. Just as he did, Princess Sundra Neeth called over to him. "Sir Seth, Sir Ollie! When we get to the castle, you must land on the roof, then follow me. I know a secret way down to the Great Hall, where the Magna Charter is kept."

Sir Seth looked over and smiled but didn't reply. He was too busy holding on to the umbie's reins with one hand and hanging on to Shasta with the other.

"Look! There's Ooz and Phi Phum just ahead of us. They're already landing on the grass in front of the castle," Sir Ollie shouted. "Boy, oh boy, this is gonna be close."

"We'll have to land on that turret at the top of the castle," Princess Sundra shouted out. "The one where the queen's blue-and-gold pennant is flying."

"Did you hear that?" Sir Seth said to Buzz as he tapped the big bird with his toes.

"Yep. Standby for landing"—Buzz started to say. Then he stopped dead and said—"uh-oh!" instead.

"'Uh-oh'? What do you mean by 'uh-oh'?" Sir Ollie immediately wanted to know from right beside them.

The umbie looked nervously over one shoulder. "I think flying is utterly grand, but, um, I'm afraid I don't know how to land!"

"Uh-oh," Sir Seth repeated.

"What are we gonna do we do now?" Sir Ollie wondered out loud.

"It's okay," Sir Seth replied. "See that long blue-and-gold pennant flappin' down there on top of that turret?"

"Yep."

"Well, the first thing we do is get our umbies to slow down as slow as they can. Then they just reach out and grab that pennant with both feet on the way by," Sir Seth said with a grin. "It's not something you'll find in the Umbie Pilot's Manual, but I think it should work. Anyhow, right now, that's the only thought that we've got. Unless you can think of a better idea in the next six seconds."

"Stand by for landing..." Sir Ollie smiled to Sir Seth and the princess.

With that, Sir Seth tapped the umbie with the tips of his toes and Buzz slowly began circling lower and lower, edging closer and closer to the long, flowing pennant. Then, when he was almost on top, Buzz stuck out both of his huge feet and grabbed not the pennant but the pole that was holding it. Which spun the umbie around and

around and around and around and
around and around the pole thirty-three
times before he came to a whizzing,
dizzying, talon-smoldering stop.

And before he or Sir Seth could
say a word, they were joined by
another crash-landing umbie.
Then another. And another.

"Well done, Mister Flyguy!"
Sir Seth grinned, patting Buzz on the
back. "You stay here. We've got work
to do." He turned to the princess.
"Now, Your Highness, where do
we go from here?"

"We must rescue the Magna Charter.
It's down in—" she began, but that's as
far as she got.

"Excuse me, but what about all the
sandwiches I was promised?" Buzz
pointedly asked. "Or are you just like
the Fibbs?"

"Where are we going to find sandwiches
up on a roof?" Sir Seth snorted.

But the princess quickly stepped in.
"See those big windows down there?
The ones still lit up?"

"Yes," the umbie said, pouting.
"What about 'em?"

"That's the kitchen. The chefs are always up before everyone else, preparing the food for the day. Go in and help yourself to whatever you want, and if anyone tries to stop you, just show them this," she said, removing an ornate jeweled ring from her finger. "This is the Coronation Ring my mother gave me to wear until the day I am crowned. Everyone in Castle Claire knows it. Now, go! There's no time to waste."

The princess turned back to the others. "Quickly, come with me. I'll show you where the Great Hall is. That's where the charter is kept!"

"Right!" cried Sir Ollie. "Let's get down there now!"

"Down?" Princess Sundra smiled slyly. "Oh no—we're going up!"

16 It's Raining Pots and Pans!

With his thin evil grin as evil and thin as it
ever had been, Ooz looked up at the queen
and Sir Duncan and pulled the Magna Charter from its
hallowed glass cask. And there, finally, was the treasured
document, firmly in his greedy, grubby little grasp…

"HAH! At long and overdue last," he sneered, "I, Ooz,
am about to be crowned the king of—"

Ooz was just about to finish this thought when—
from somewhere high overhead—a heavy iron frying
pan interrupted him instead, arriving with quite a loud
KAH-BONGGGGG!! squarely on top of Ooz's
still-grinning head.

"Now, Sir Seth. NOW!" Princess Sundra's voice
echoed down and around and around from the top of the
Great Hall.

From out of nowhere—and before the woozy, wobbling Ooz had time to react—the streaking tinfoil figure of Sir Seth Thistlethwaite swung out across the huge hall on the long golden cord that Queen Beatrix the Sixth usually used to summon afternoon tea. Flashing past all the startled guards, he cleanly scooped the Magna Charter right out of the still-woozy Ooz's still-grubby little hand! All as smoothly as if he'd been swinging down into Puddlewater Pond.

"Sir Ollie! Over to you!" Sir Seth called out as he passed the charter to his friend, who came swinging down from the balcony, heading the other way.

With the cherished charter clasped firmly in one hand, Sir Ollie called up to the princess, "Ready, Your Highness? Here comes the charter!"

"Ready!" she called back
from her hiding place high up at
the top of the hall.

Sir Ollie swung back up to the balcony that ran
around the front wall of the Great Hall, where Shasta
stood eagerly waiting. Sir Ollie quickly slid the treasured
piece of parchment into a long blue-and-gold velvet
sleeve and knotted the golden cord at the top, then gave
it to Shasta, who, with a big happy smile—the way only
certain horses can do—took off at the gallop down the
long candle-lit hall to the winding carpeted stairway at
the far end. Shasta ran up the stairs two at a time until
she was almost at the top.

And that's when their plan began to fall apart.

Shasta was just one step from the top when her four
furiously flying feet suddenly got tangled in the golden
cord—and she dropped the Magna Charter!

If that wasn't dire and disastrous enough, the cherished
charter slipped out of the sleeve as it tumbled back down
the stairs! Before Shasta could grab it, a passing whiff
of wind came wafting down the hall, caught the elusive
piece of parchment, and tumbled it lazily end over end
all the way out, out, and over the Great Hall, where it
flipped and flopped in its slow-going way down, down,
down—toward Ooz's hazy helmeted head!

"Guards! Guards!" Queen Beatrix shouted in her usual chandelier-shattering shriek. "Grab the charter before it gets to Ooz."

Everyone in the Great Hall just stood there, so shaken and shocked they couldn't believe what their surprised eyes were seeing.

"Sir Seth!" Sir Ollie shouted. "Red alert! Shasta just dropped the charter! It's floating back down toward Ooz!"

From the far side of the Great Hall, Sir Seth instantly sprang into action. Without his even having to take time to think, his Mighty Knightly instincts took over. First, he ran to the wall of the Great Hall and grabbed one of the long pointed spears from the queen's coat of arms. Then he swung out over Ooz and snagged the treasured charter from midair by the thick golden cord at the top! He looked up to the balcony for his friend.

"Ready, Sir Ollie?" he called.

"Ready!" Sir Ollie replied.

"Okay! Comin' atcha!"

With a mighty heave, Sir Seth threw the charter-carrying spear as hard as he could up to the balcony where Sir Ollie was waiting. Well, almost up to the balcony. The long spear was heavier than Sir Seth had thought—instead of landing on the balcony, it glanced off the mahogany railing and then dropped straight down where it landed on top of Ooz's head with another loud, resounding...

KAH-BONGGGGG!!

Which sent the evil little elf into dizzy daze all over again!

"Sir Ollie, quick! Swing down now and grab it!"

"On my waaaaay!" Sir Ollie said, as he launched himself off the balcony.

As he did, Sir Seth looked all the way up to the glass dome at the top of the Great Hall. "Your Highness!" he called up to the princess.

"Yes?" she called back.

"Sir Ollie's on his way up with the charter. You know this castle better than anyone else! Stash it some place where it'll be safe—somewhere no one will find it!"

"I know just the place!" she called back.

Finally, Sir Ollie reached out, and once again, the travel-weary Magna Charter was scooped from the top of Ooz's head. Then Sir Ollie swung back up to the balcony, where Shasta was still sitting, eagerly waiting.

"C'mon, girl, take this up to the princess," he said quickly.

Shasta sat up and barked twice, which meant she understood.

Sir Ollie slid the parchment back into the velvet sleeve, then put it in Shasta's mouth. "Okay, off you go..."

Shasta took off up the stairs as though her tail were on fire.

"Hey, Shasta!" Sir Ollie suddenly called out.

Shasta stopped dead in her tracks and looked back at Sir Ollie.

He smiled his good old Sir Ollie smile and said, "This time, watch that top step."

Shasta almost barked back a thank-you but caught herself just in time—and double-wagged her tail instead. Then turned and took off out of sight.

By the time the thoroughly confused little Ooz was finally coming to and rubbing the bump on his head, Princess Sundra had the precious document safely stowed in the left arm of Sir Cecil's suit of armor outside the anteroom at the main entrance of the castle!

"Good girl, Shasta," Princess Sundra said, scratching Shasta on the head. "Now, come with me. There's just one more thing we must do."

Shasta grinned up at the princess and followed her back to the Great Hall, where Sir Seth and Sir Ollie were already waiting.

"Good work, my fine shiny friends!" Princess Sundra smiled, then turned to Ooz and her mother. "You will be pleased to know, the Magna Charter is safely hidden away where only I will be able to find it. And there shall it stay until my own coronation."

The queen cleared her throat. "Well, now that the Magna Charter is safely hidden away and my daughter is clearly no longer in danger, I suggest there's still some unfinished business to be discussed," she said, looking directly at the Ooz. "Such as what we're going to do about Mister Ooz and his tree-eating friend."

Realizing he had just been roundly and soundly

defeated—and not knowing what sort of fate was about to befall him—Ooz didn't feel nearly as evil or quite as awful as he had a few moments before.

"HAH!" he growled, bruised but unbeaten. "You can do whatever you want! But just remember, you'll be doin' it without any water if you don't turn Claire over to me!"

"I think not, Mister Ooz!" Queen Beatrix said firmly, increasing the tension one level more. "Guards! Seize him!"

Immediately, the uniformed guards surrounded the evil little elf. Then the queen stepped forward, raised both arms, and solemnly proclaimed: "For your treasonous and unreasoned actions against the fair Queendom of Claire, on this day, in the reign of Queen Beatrix the Sixth, be it known to one and all that the evil, awful elf known as Ooz and the Snactisaurus rex known as Grak have both been banished to the Outlands! For ever and ever. Or for all eternity. Whichever comes first."

Ooz snarled like a mad dog as he was led outside by Claire's royal guards. "You think you can get rid of us as easy as that? HAH!"

"Us?" repeated the queen. "To what 'us' are you referring exactly?"

Ooz was about to answer when he looked around. Phi and her condor had flown away. And even he had no idea where Grak was. And so Ooz, that disgusting little elf, could only let out a snort of shame.

Sir Seth leaned over to the princess. "So what are the Outlands?"

"Nobody knows," she whispered back. "They're way out beyond the Sadlands—so far away, nobody who's been there has ever come back."

Sir Ollie quickly turned to the princess and whispered, "Hey, Your Highness, what does 'banished' mean?"

"It means 'sent away forever.'"

Then Sir Ollie turned and whispered to Sir Seth, "Y'know, maybe we should get banished, too. It might be the only way we're ever gonna get home."

Sir Seth looked at his friend and smiled. "Why? Is it suppertime already?"

The princess obviously heard what he said. "You want to go to the Outlands with Ooz?" she gasped. "Why would you want to do that?"

Sir Ollie just shrugged. "How else are we ever gonna get home? We can't get back up through the hole in the sky. The Outlands might be our only way out." He turned back to Sir Seth. "What do you think?"

Sir Seth thought about it quickly. "I think you're right. We can't go up. There's no other way."

Sir Ollie turned to the princess. "Uh, what's down the other way, at the other end of Claire?"

"A wall."

"A wall?"

Princess Sundra Neeth held up both arms. "Yes. A wall. It reaches right up to the sky."

"Uh, what's on the other side of the wall?"

"More wall, I guess." Princess Sundra Neeth smiled.

Sir Ollie had made up his mind. "Then the Outlands are the only way out."

Sir Seth nodded, then looked up at the queen. "Your Majesty, as Mighty Knights errant, Sir Ollie and Shasta and I would be honored to escort Ooz and Grak to the Outlands—to make sure that they get there."

The queen walked over to the Mighty Knights and Shasta. "You're leaving? How can the Queendom of Claire ever thank you for all you have done?"

"Thank us?" Sir Seth blushed. "Heck, it was fun! Right, everyone?"

The queen and the council of elders and everyone else enthusiastically agreed.

"But before you go on your way, you will be happy to know that with Ooz and Grak defeated, I will instruct the royal engineers to draw up plans to unblock the River Claire...and take down our pipeline up to the clouds."

"Thank you, Your Majesty. King Philip Fluster the Fourth will be glad to hear that!" Sir Ollie sighed.

"It is our pleasure, good sir knight," said the queen smiling. "The Mighty Knights have indeed proved their word and their worth to the people of Claire. Thank you for restoring order once again to our queendom."

"Okay, come on, Mighty Knights! We've got a long way to go," Sir Seth said, taking Princess Sundra Neeth by the hand. "Your Highness, I guess this means you can turn the Sadlands back into the Gladlands again."

"It will be the first thing our queendom does," she smiled back. "And Sir Seth?"

"Yes?" he said, turning back.

"I apologize for dropping that water bomb on your head."

Sir Seth grinned from ear to ear. "That's okay. I apologize for putting a frog under your pillow on the way down to the Great Hall just now."

"Under my pillow?"

"Well, I sure *hope* it was your pillow."

17 Over and Outlands

The sand became deeper and deeper as Sir Seth and Sir Ollie rode their umbies, escorting the banished Ooz and Grak farther and farther into the barren sandy Outlands, until there was almost nothing around them at all but sand. Except for over there, where a few jagged rocks formed what seemed to be the foothills of a mountain.

Sir Seth slid down from his perch on top of his under-umbie and wearily sat down, then he turned to Ooz, the evil little elf. "Well, Mister Ooz, this looks like the far edge of the Outlands. This is where we leave you. I hope you like your new home."

Ooz grunted but didn't look up.

Grak said nothing at all.

Then Sir Ollie slid down from his under-umbie and handed Ooz a large blue-and-gold velvet sack he had tied to the back of his umbie. "This is for you," he said, looking Ooz straight in the eye. "Use them wisely. They could save your life."

"Right!" Sir Seth agreed. "And I brought a bag along for Grak."

Even Shasta dropped another large velvet bag at their feet.

Ooz looked at all three bags, then back at the two knights. "What's this?" he growled.

"They're acorns," Sir Ollie said.

"And chestnuts," Sir Seth added.

"And a bagful of seeds for birch trees and elm trees, plus a few cherry berries and some peach and pear trees, too. Hundreds and hundreds of them," they both said together.

"We got them from the forests around the castle," explained Sir Seth. "Now that you're out here in the Outlands, if you plant them, you'll live. If Grak eats them, you'll die. The choice, Mister Ooz, is completely up to you."

"Just like it was back there in Claire," Sir Ollie added.

Then from out of nowhere, one more voice suddenly joined the chorus. "Uh, I'd like you to meet someone…"

"Glug?!" Sir Seth gasped, completely surprised. "Where did you come from?"

"We live here, remember?" Glug, the chuggamugga bug, shrugged. "The Sadlands and the Outlands are all the same to us, really. We're just the only creatures with enough water on hand to make the trip! Anyway, this is Slug, one of my two hundred and twenty-two thousand, two hundred and two cousins who live here," he grinned. "Slug, this is Ooz. We want you to know that the chuggamuggas just took a vote: we'll water these seeds for you. The way we see it, this could be the only chance we ever get to turn all this sand into green trees and grass again."

"Sounds like a plan," Sir Ollie agreed. "But that's up

to Ooz and Grak to decide."

Ooz didn't bother to even look up or grunt.

Sir Ollie just shrugged. "Well, Glug, we tried, but now whatever happens here is up to you two."

"Yep," Sir Seth agreed. "Goodbye, Mister Ooz. And you, too, Grak."

"Goodbye, you guys," Grak's voice replied sadly from way up high. "And I just want you to know, before you go, that I'm never, never, never gonna eat another pea or tree or knight ever again. That's a promise."

The two Mighty Knights stopped dead in their tracks and turned to look back. "A promise?"

"Yep. A promise," Grak eagerly agreed.

Sir Seth and Sir Ollie walked over to the huge dino and looked up in awe. "Remember—a promise is a promise," Sir Seth reminded him.

"No matter what. Right?" Sir Ollie added.

"Right!" Grak agreed again. "No matter what."

"Great! But, uh, what are you going to eat instead?" Sir Ollie wondered.

A twinkle appeared in the corner of Grak's eye. "Well, those Fibbs and I were talking back at the cave, and I've decided that from now on, I'm gonna eat nothing but..."

"Yes?" the Mighty Knights said, leaning forward in breathless anticipation.

"SAND!"

"Sand!" Sir Seth gagged at the thought.

"Sand?" Sir Ollie gagged in agreement. "That sounds pretty ucky to me."

"Ucky? Good heavens no!" Grak grinned and inhaled a huge mouthful of sand. "Sadlands sand is utterly scrumdillyicious ducky. It tastes like anything I want it to be."

"Yeah?" Sir Seth shuddered at the thought. "Well, it sure sounds pretty crunchy and scrunchy to me."

Grak took another monster mouthful of sand. "Then you haven't tried my superb Saharan Sandfly Souffle. Or my dreamy, creamy Kalahari Calamari. Or perhaps some nice Gobi Anchovie Pot Pie is more to your taste..."

Sir Seth grinned at Sir Ollie. "Or maybe even meatloaf SANDwiches...like the ones my mother makes."

That did it! Sir Ollie sighed a homesick sort of sigh. "Come on, Sir Seth. It's time to go home."

EPILOGUE
The Way Home?

As they soared higher and higher into the brightening sky, the travel-weary umbies rounded the marbled two-mile-high wall at the mouth of the underground caverns of Claire, and instantly, dazzling yellow sunlight streamed down through a yawning opening overhead.

"Y'know what?" said Sir Seth, shielding his eyes.

"No. What?" Sir Ollie replied.

"I think this is the way in—and the way out," he beamed. "By golly, Sir Ollie, we're on our way home!"

"Good!" Sir Ollie beamed right back. "'Cause I have to be home before the streetlights come on, don't forget."

Sir Seth reached around Shasta and patted Buzz on the back on his head. "Do you want to come to Thatchwych with us—or are you going back home to Claire?"

Buzz looked over one shoulder. "Well, I've sure had a ton of fun with you guys, and I'll never, never, ever forget you... but home is home. So I guess that's where I'll go."

Sir Seth sighed sort of sadly. "Okay, well, when we get through that opening up there, look around for a place to land. Sir Ollie and I will go on foot from there."

The two big birds climbed up, up, up through the gaping mouth of the caves—out into a suddenly and surprisingly double-dazzling world of white snow!

Buzz looked around and found a flat place to land. He circled lower and lower, then put out his feet and skidded to a stop—all with his enormous nose stuck in four feet of fluffy white snow! Quite a nasty, frosty shock for someone who lives in the desert.

"Goodbye, you g-g-guys," Buzz shivered. "I'm g-g-going home to get w-w-warm!"

With that, the awkward umbies began their bumbling, stumbling run with wings spread wide and began to fly. They circled around, swooped down, and with a wave of their wings, headed back to the opening of the caves.

"I don't remember it snowing when we left Thatchwych, Sir Ollie," said Sir Seth, looking around.

"WelcometoAhAhKaachu!" a tiny, lightning-like voice welcomed them from somewhere nearby.

Sir Seth looked at Sir Ollie. "Did you just hear someone say something?"

"Yeah. It sounded like 'Welcome to Ah Ah Kaachu' or something," Sir Ollie agreed. "Only really, really fast."

"Where's Ah Ah Kaachu?" Sir Seth asked the invisible voice, looking all around.

"You'realreadythere, sowhydoyouask?" the little voice said just as quickly as before.

"We were sorta hoping this was Thatchwych," Sir Ollie sighed, slumping forlornly in the snow. "Now what, Sir Seth? Here we are in a whole new 'nuther place where we don't know where we are. We're never gonna get home!"

There was a tiny pause as the little voice thought about what Sir Ollie had said. "Didyoujustsay'Thatchwych'?"

"Yes!" the two knights said, whirling around together excitedly. "Do you know where it is?"

"Nope. Afraidnot."

Sir Ollie was still trying to locate the voice. "Excuse me, little buddy, but where are you? And who are you?"

"Jabberjaws, theblabbermouse. MessengeroftheIceMice," said Jabberjaws in warp-speed Squeakspeak—the official language of the Ice Mice. "I'monyourfoot. Butyoucan'tsee me'causeI'mtoowhite. Andtoosmall. Whoareyou?"

Now, in case you haven't already guessed, Ice Mice speak so very, very quickly that every sentence they speak sounds just like one long, long squeak. But Jabberjaws squeakspeaks even faster than that. Which is why he's the messenger of the Ice Mice. And if you think he speaks quickly, wait until see him run!

"I'm Sir Ollie Everghettz. And this is Sir Seth Thistlethwaite and his faithful steed—" Sir Ollie began until he was excitedly interrupted by Jabberjaws.

"Wow! TheMightyKnightsofRightandHonor! ThatSirSethandthatSirOllie?"

Sir Seth perked up. "Yes. Why do you ask?"

Jabberjaws jumped up onto Sir Ollie's nose, where Sir Ollie could see him. "Ihaveareally, reallyimportant messageforyou."

"You do? From who?"

"TheFaerieQueenofAhAhKaachu," Jabberjaws said quickly. "We'vebeentryingtofindyouforweeks."

"Faerie Queen? Of Ah Ah Kaachu?" wondered Sir Seth.

"Why does she wanna see us?"

Jabberjaws shuddered all over. "TohelpusfightBetty!"

"To, uh, fight Betty? Who's Betty?"

At the mere mention of her name, Jabberjaws shuddered all over—all over again. "BettytheYeti! She'svery, veryscary. Ialmostfaintedjustsayinghername."

Sir Seth leaned over to see the little mouse better. "What's so bad about Betty?"

"Everything!" Jabberjaws squeaked excitedly. "She'striple-awfulevil...timesten!"

"Triple-awful evil?" Sir Ollie echoed.

"Times ten?" Sir Seth gasped. "That's ten times badder than bad ever gets. How does she get this bad?"

The little mouse pointed nervously to the top of the mountain. "Seeallthatsnowupthere?"

Sir Seth and Sir Ollie both looked all the way up to the top of the Rhee Li Hai Mountains. "Yeah."

"Well, Betty'sgoingtodumpitalldownhereonus!" panted Jabberjaws. "She'llburythetownunderanavalanche!"

Now it was Sir Ollie's turn to shudder. "Why?"

Jabberjaws shrugged. "Shejustlikesbeingtriple-awfulevil, Iguess."

Sir Seth drew his sword and held it high. "By golly, Sir Ollie, if we're stuck here, it may as well be on a whole new Mighty Knights adventure! To arms!"

"OK, Sir Seth," Sir Ollie agreed. "I'm with you. Let's show Betty the Yeti just how bad bad really can get!"

Just how bad is Betty the Yeti?
Can Sir Seth and Sir Ollie
survive the suffocating snow and
awful avalanches to face her and
save the people of Ah Ah Kaachu?
And will the Mighty Knights ever
make it back home?

COMING IN 2012

SIR SETH
THISTLETHWAITE

Meets Betty the Yeti

"To Claire, who constantly reminds me how much fun it is to be a kid."

Richard Thake

Richard began his writing career at Maclean-Hunter Publishing Company in Toronto in 1958. He later moved into the advertising business, creating award-winning campaigns for many well-known corporations, and became the associate creative director of one of Canada's largest advertising agencies. A father of three grown children and a grandfather of three, Richard has finally found the time to write the Sir Seth series—a thinly disguised glimpse into his own "theater of the mind" childhood adventures with his friends in the Don River Valley and the Beach areas of Toronto.

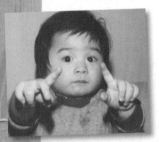

Vince Chui

Vince has spent the last six years creating illustrations and concept artwork for various entertainment properties. While at Pseudo Interactive, he worked on Xbox 360, Playstation 3, and PS2 games. Since then, he's moved on to do work with other industry staples, including Sega and Paramount Pictures. He enjoys character design—when he's not out playing Ultimate Frisbee.